Real for Me

KIA,

Real for Me

A Novel by Eric E. Pete

THANKS FOR ALL THE LOVE & SUPPORT OVER THE YEARS. IT TOUCHES MY HEART.

Eric Pete
AUG 1, 2009

E-fect Publishing
HARVEY, LOUISIANA
www.e-fectpublishing.com

This book is a work of fiction. Names, characters, places and events are products of the author's imagination or are used fictitiously. Any resemblance to actual events, locations or persons, living or deceased, is purely coincidental. We assume no responsibility for errors, inaccuracies, omissions, or any inconsistency herein.

First printing 2001

ISBN 0-9704995-2-3

LCCN 00-135804

ATTENTION CORPORATIONS, UNIVERSITIES, COLLEGES, AND PROFESSIONAL ORGANIZATIONS: Quantity discounts are available on bulk purchases of this book for educational, gift purposes, or as premiums for increasing magazine subscriptions or renewals. Special books or book excerpts can also be created to fit specific needs. For information, please contact E-fect Publishing, PO Box 2425, Harvey, LA 70059-2425, ph 504-433-1727; www.e-fectpublishing.com.

Acknowledgments

Well, well, well. My first acknowledgments section . . . but not my last. Let's get to it, shall we?

First of all, a special thanks to my divine muse, God, who created my "spark" and guided me on my journey. Much Love.

To my first fans, Shontea Smith, Sherita Forbes, and Veronica "Ronnie" Bridgewater. I'll never forget that night y'all were talkin' to the computer screen! You just don't know how much that meant to me. Sherita, your card and kind words meant a lot.

To my "mystery readers"—Shontea Smith(again), Natalie Lumpkin-Brown (Sea-town! Wha! Wha!), Jamie Lemonier, Angela Keyes, Carmel Johnson, Jackie Simien, Karen Pinnix (Congrats on the baby!), and Judith "Jaye" Bostic. You guys are da bomb! Thanks for the words of encouragement and constructive criticism.

To fellow authors and new friends, Eric Jerome Dickey, Troy Martin, and Tajuana "TJ" Butler, thanks for being so approachable and for welcoming a brother into the fold. It was cool just kickin' it with y'all. You guys are role models to the rest of us and are a shining example of what others can achieve with hard work, determination, and persistence.

Jhay Davis-you da man! You took my initial sketches/roughs and ran with it. Thank you for the beautiful cover design! (Check out Jhay's website at www.neoxecutive.com!)

To my cousins, Norlin and Bernice Evans. Your help in the beginning was priceless. Told ya I wouldn't forget!

To my little girl, Chelsea. Just because. Love da baby!

To my mother, Edna Mae. A role model of kindness and love for all. Your baby boy loves you.

To Lake Charles, LA and the Los Angeles area. Holler if you hear me!

To Monica Pierre, another fellow author, radio personality, inspirational source, and all-around good person, thank you for sharing.

To all my co-workers who were my daily support system, thanks for believing in me. You know who you are.

To Unit 530, past and present, thanks!

All my friends and family, unnamed, who offered support and encouragement, thanks for being there.

To Jan Clifford of Barnes & Noble, Denise Walter-McConduit, and anyone else that I may have missed, luv ya! Believe me, any omissions were unintentional.

"Thank you for choosing Eric E. Pete airlines. Buckle up. The ride is just beginning."

1   *Glover McDaniel*

Beeeeeeeeeeeep! Beeeeeeeeeeeep! Beeeeeeeeeeeeeeep! Beeeeeeeeeeeeeeeep!

"Shit! Why did the alarm have to go off right when I was about to get *my* groove on? I guess Taye would have to catch me on the next dream go-round."

Damn, I hate Mondays. I really don't feel like going to work today, but then I never feel like going to work. Lionel mentioned it again last night. That was just before I made him go home. Some women out here would jump at the chance to have someone like Lionel take care of them, but "Hey!" . . . I guess I'm just a strong, independent Black woman. Did I forget sexy, vivacious, witty, intelligent, and a *damn* good lay? Haha!

Lionel is my boyfriend/fiancée. I say that because we're not officially engaged. We met over 2 years ago by chance, when I was going through one of my dry spells. I was at Mariana's having a chicken caesar salad after work and he was downtown meeting with a client. I was sitting there feeding my face and saw this rather debonair brother at a nearby table. He was a tall, dark-skinned brother with a medium build, bald head, and good teeth and his suit obviously set him back a little. He was having a business meeting with a middle-aged white man who appeared to be interested in more than "bid'ness" as was evident by the way he was eyeing the brother. I was hoping to myself, "Please

1

don't be gay!" and suddenly realized that I was eyeing Mr. Chocolate as well.

Their business was concluded when the client signed some paperwork. The client left first and passed right by my table. Lionel was passing next when he slowed and mumbled under his breath, "Thought that was funny, huh?" I almost choked on a crouton.

"Excuse me?"

"I saw you watching my predicament. You seemed to be amused watching me deal with Mr. Brewster."

"Oh. That. Well . . . I"

"And the answer is 'no', I'm not gay."

Phew!

Lionel sat down and introduced himself to me and the rest is history.

Lionel is a securities broker and financial planner for Barnes & Greenwood and is doing very well for himself. We started dating steady a few months after Mariana's. Lionel has asked me countless times to move in with him, but I don't want to shack up (although we do spend the night at each other's place from time to time). I also have some reservations without a wedding date being picked and all. I'm pretty sure I love him, but want to be certain that the weekend trips to San Diego, Catalina, etc. aren't swaying me instead. We're going to have a long talk soon, but first let me get my ass out of this bed and get ready for work before Mona gets here. Heaven knows Mona's gonna get me evicted with her loud honking!

2 _Maxwell "Max" Guillory_

While Glover was preparing for work at her L.A. apartment on Vicente Boulevard, there was another scene developing a few miles away on Venice Boulevard this morning. The theme song from Shaft was bellowing through the walls from above Max's one bedroom apartment . . . Smitty's normal morning routine. Sade's "Smooth Operator" graced Max's ears as he prepared a light breakfast of oatmeal and orange juice. A strange chorus of " . . . coast to coast, L.A. to Chicago . . ." was being intermingled with "you daaaaamn right" from Smitty's system upstairs. Still, Smitty's little ass was the closest thing to a best friend out here since moving to the City of Angels from little Lake Charles, Louisiana over six months ago.

Maxwell Guillory had graduated from McNeese State University with a BS in business administration over two years ago. He had decided to work locally in Lake Charles on one of the gambling riverboats as a slot attendant and had saved up a nest egg before embarking west. Max had considered moving to Houston, but he wanted to get as far away as possible to avoid being "sucked back" into Lake Charles as so many friends had. Max had learned from his college professors that all paths to success led out of Lake Charles and that mobility was the key to a higher standard of living. Of course Max's mother, Orelia, didn't want to hear that noise. She wanted her baby to stay close to home.

3

Max was the spitting image of his father who had died in a chemical plant explosion when Max was in the third grade and Orelia clung to her memories. Orelia was calmed by the fact that her brother and his family resided in Carson, so Max would have some family in the area to look out for him.

Rinnnnnnnng! Max picked up his phone.

"Hello?"

"What up *Maxwell*?" It was Smitty. Max hated the way Smitty called him by his full name while stressing the last syllable.

"Smitty, I know you the man and all, but you need to turn that Shaft shit down this early in the a.m.!"

"Hey! You know me! It helps get a brother motivated after a long night of dealing with the womens! You know I'm a baddddddddd mother- . . . "

"Shut your mouth!" Hahaha!

"You ready to go check on jobs?"

"Yeah. I started to come downstairs earlier and knock on your door, but decided to check out Mrs. Barnes doing her morning laps in the pool!"

"Awwww!!!! . . . and you didn't come get me! Fuck you!"

"Yeah. Right! Like you would know what to do if she approached you! You know Fistina & Palmetta are the only women for you lately!"

"Fuck you, Smit!"

"Be right down, baby! Haha!"

3 *Glover*

Mona had pulled up late and honking as usual in her gold Mazda 626. Mona was the daughter of a successful real estate agent who made his money reinvesting in the inner city. She was a brown-skinned, leggy twenty-six year old with a cute little tapered short crop who severely disliked her stepmother. Mona's dad put her up in a comfy little condo in Santa Monica as a way of making up for his new trophy wife. Mona wasn't stupid so she did take the "gift" although she usually avoided letting Dad do her any favors. Mona made the most of her 5'6" petite yet curvy frame, which was pretty devastating when combined with her smooth, sophisticated voice and good looks.

Mona and I had been best friends for about six years. We attended community college together at West Los Angeles College. When I landed the job at the downtown state employment office, I brought her along about a month later. We were as close as sisters and tried to look out for one another as if we were.

"So did Lionel spend the night last night?", Mona asked as I was digging in my purse for lipstick during the drive in to work.

"Naahhh. Had to send the nigger home last night. You know I'm not ready for all of that. . . besides I had to get *some* sleep!"

"You know, you really need to stop using the n-word, Ms. McDaniel. There was this big thing on TV last night about that."

"You watch too much TV, Mona."

5

"Don't I though!? Anyway. Have you guys had the talk yet?"

"No, but we need to. I've been holding off bringing it up. You still messing around with Craig?"

"Oh . . . changing the subject, Ms. McDaniel?"

"Nope. Just making conversation. Are we still going out this weekend?"

"I guess. Have you checked with Charmaine?"

Charmaine was our co-worker at the employment office who happened to be Caucasian on the outside, but was total sister on the inside. Hell, she was even built like a sister! Charmaine grew up around minorities most of her life and had even experienced some of the same ups and downs. She always kept us laughing around work and always knew the latest scuttlebutt around the office. Charmaine, Mona, and I usually had our "sister-time" every weekend when we would go out and unwind. Sometimes we just hung out at one of our apartments and sipped coolers while exhaling.

Traffic was unusually light this morning on the way downtown and we even made it in on time. Mona parked next to Charmaine's black Hyundai Sonata on the parking lot behind the office. Charmaine was spotted right after Mona and I had clocked in. She had her hands full with French toast sticks and a cup of coffee, but that didn't stop her from running up.

"G-love! Mona!"

Her own little pet name for me was a play on the spelling of my name and very original even though I hated the fuck out of it.

"Did you guys see those brothers working out in front of the Times building? Dammmnnnn! I might have to take a little walk at lunch! Haha!"

"Good morning to you too, Charmaine!"

"Charmaine, are we going out this weekend?"

"You know, G-love! You know! You've got Lionel and Ms. Mona here has . . . well . . . I don't know who she has this week, but I've got to play catch up!"

"Whatever," Mona said in a dry tone. "I really don't date that much."

"I don't know what you call it, but you do do it much!"

Mona shot Charmaine the bird. This sort of playful exchange between Ms. Yin and Ms. Yang went on all day and helped time pass.

4

Max

Smitty and I had decided to spend the first half of the day pounding the pavement in search of well paying jobs. I had spent my time in Los Angeles getting acclimated and working odd jobs, but hadn't found anything to lead to my pot of gold yet. I was working evenings at Denny's on Hawthorne in Torrance, but was off today. My nest egg was beginning to run a little low and the last thing I was going to do was call Orelia for some money. I could hear her now telling me to come home. Although my major was in business, I did have some computer experience and was an assistant in the computer lab at business school. I hoped to try to combine the two into something productive.

We took my Celica as Smitty was without wheels at the time. Smitty's hooptie was always broken, but he always managed to find some sweet young thang to either ride him around or allow him to borrow their wheels. They weren't always the most appealing of prospects, but Smitty really didn't seem to mind. "I gets minez!!!!!", he would always say.

Smitty was one of the first people I met upon moving to Los Angeles. Matter of fact, it was his damn Shaft music that did it. It was my second day after finding my apartment on Venice Boulevard with the help of my cousin, Jay. I was crashing hard after being up all night unpacking and putting away my stuff. Shaft's theme song came blaring from above and went through the walls and right through my head waking me up. I was banging up on the ceiling for a few minutes, but to no avail. I threw on some clothes and went running up the stairwell in search of someone to punch out. I banged on Smitty's door and wasn't expecting to see this skinny little figure looking at me when the door opened. He actually had the look on his face like he was being disturbed. This 5'5 bird-chested individual in a silk robe was such a sight to behold that my eyes watered up while holding back a laugh.

All I could think of was, "that Shaft's a bad mother- . . ."

Smitty replied, "Shut your mouth!" and we fell out laughing in the hallway. We've been hanging ever since.

We hit the end of town northeast of L.A. from Pasadena to around Pomona. Applications were filled out, resumes were dropped off, and even some brief interviews and handshakes were given, but nothing definite. After working hard at trying to get work, we had promised to get some playing time in. I had the evening off from Denny's. We changed clothes in the restroom at the last place we had hit and got back on I-10 to head to Venice for some b-ball.

It was our usual ritual. We managed to get on the court after an hour and lost both games. That didn't stop Smitty from talking shit. Smitty, being a little man, had to always talk shit. This was true whether it was our b-ball games at Venice or the flag football we got involved in on weekends. Usually it amused the other participants as Smitty thought he was the Second Coming. We always hated to burst his bubble.

Smitty and I retreated to the Third Street Promenade in Santa Monica to lick our wounds and found an outdoor seat at one of the bar and grills. Smitty ordered the chicken strips and fries with a beer. I ordered the fajitas and was nursing a margarita.

" . . . next Kobe."

"Say what, Smitty?!"

"Next Kobe, Max. I'm telling ya. I'm gonna be the next Kobe. You saw me out there."

"So maybe you shouldn't have bothered job searching with me today. Or did your royal Kobeness do that just to keep me company?"

"Don't hate on the brother like those fools back at Venice. You saw all the elbows whenever I drove!"

"Yeah. How are the chicken strips?"

"They're awight. The longneck's helping though. It cost enough. How's your shit?"

"Pretty good actually. I need to get paid though so I can start eating some high-end shit. Y'know. Filet mignon . . . "

" . . . Prime rib! Yeah dawg! I hear ya! You're gonna have an easier time with your Bachelors degree, even if it is from down south. My Associate should help me at least get a decent set of wheels. Brotherman's getting tired of bummin'."

"All in due time, Smit. We need to hit downtown next week and look for the job hookup."

"Hey Max, shorties at three o'clock."

Smitty's radar had come on. There were two blondes who had just sat down a few tables over from us. Judging from the crowd that had just picked up; they'd probably just left the movies down the street. The taller one was a dirty blonde with a short frizzy hairstyle and was pretty well endowed. She was sporting a black halter-top with a pair of flared Gap denims. The short one had straight, shoulder length hair with ass for days. She was wearing a white designer T-shirt with a pair of shorts that highlighted her "assets". It was a little cool for shorts, especially those shorts, but this was California. I was still adjusting to that. Diversity at its finest.

"So, are we gonna do this dawg? The short one's callin' to me!"

"Smitty, you don't even know if they're game. Besides, we're all sweaty and shit."

"Hey! Sweat now! Sweat later! Does it matter?"

It had been too long.

5 _Glover_

This Monday at the California Employment Development Office was a little busier than usual. New state requirements had come down along with a plethora of new forms, etc. Charmaine was in charge of filing so the day was wearing even on her usually upbeat, devil-may-care attitude. Mona had been confirming employment searches of benefit recipients who sometimes creeped her out and I was doing a little bit of everything. During our first break we managed to chat some more.

"These mutherfuckers are gonna make me go postal in here."

"Girl please, you'd be on lock-down so quick . . . ," replied Mona to Charmaine.

"Oooo lock-down! At a male prison I would hope," said Charmaine.

"Please no prison talk this early in the day ladies!"

"Speaking of prison G-love . . . what's been going on with you and Mr. Moneybags?"

"If you're talking about Lionel, Charmaine, we are still dating and _stuff_. In fact, we're having lunch today."

"What I mean, Glover, is Lionel going to make you an honest woman? Hmmmm?"

"I'm as honest as they come already, girl. I don't need some man to make me honest."

"I heard that," chimed in Mona. "Girl, let Glover do her thang!"

"Honestly, we really haven't discussed the marriage issue that much. I mean, Lionel appears to be interested, but he's not pressuring me (much). He has been asking me to move in with him and quit my job . . . "

"Quit your job!?!?!? And you haven't skipped out yet on this place?" Charmaine was flabbergasted. "Girl, I would have told everyone in here to kiss my white ass! Especially Mr. Marx!"

Mr. Marx was the office supervisor and Charmaine hated him with a passion, but still needed her job so she nervously looked around the break room to ensure he wasn't within earshot.

"That's why she's with Lionel and you're not Charmaine," chimed in Mona. "Glover's strong and independent."

"Thank you, my sister! I gotta give you a high five on that one! I'd love to stay and chat, but this independent sister has work to do before I meet my man for lunch. "

Lionel and I met up for lunch at New Japan Sushi Bar downtown in Little Tokyo. I was waiting in front when Lionel pulled up in his Volvo. There was the large lunchtime crowd, but the service was fast. I was still new to some of the stuff Lionel was exposing me to. I wimped out with the shrimp tempura lunch while Lionel went with the raw salmon sushi and vegetable rolls. Lionel's work schedule had been up and down lately so we hadn't been having our lunches as frequently as when we first met. Lionel was wearing one of his power suits, a single breasted charcoal Antonini Loretta with a white silk shirt and designer tie. Something Mona would have picked out.

"You are looking good today, woman. How's your day going?" Lionel was giving me that look.

"It's going. That's about it. Busier than usual. I missed you last night."

"Oh really? Then why'd you make me leave?" Lionel was giving me the puppy dog look.

"You know how that goes, Lionel. Gotta keep you wanting more!"

"Oh, I want alright!"

Lionel had a little piece of veggie roll dangling on the corner of his mouth. I took that time to lean over the table and remove it while stealing a juicy kiss. Lionel was quick to accept the kiss and returned one of his own. A slight chill ran down my back as memories of last night creeped back into my consciousness.

"Is that a new suit?"

"Yeah. I picked it up last week. Antonini Loretta. You like?"

"It's nice. Kind of like Mona's style. I'm a little less into the Italian stuff."

"How is Mona doing? . . . and Charmaine? They're still carrying on at your office? "

"You know how they are. Some things will never change. We're supposed to go out this weekend . . . want to come? You haven't been out with us in a while."

"Uh. Well, I would but I have a presentation to do for the big boss next week. Want to come by tomorrow night?"

"Sure . . . but I'm not spending the night, Lionel."

"Awww, Glover!!!!"

The waitress came to our table to bring the check and to clean up.

"*Domo arigatozaimasu*, Keiko," said Lionel in his usual smooth manner.

"Thank you Mr. Dunning," replied the waitress with just a hint of an accent.

"Come here often?"

"Every now and then since it is in the area. I meet some customers here for business sometimes . . . kind of like at Mariana's that time."

"Yep. I will never forget that! Is Mr. Brewster still your account? Haha!"

"No!" chuckled Lionel. "Misha at the office has it now. Remember her?"

"Oh yeah! The Greek chick? Kinda eager-beaver? Really perky?"

"Haha! Yeah, that's her. She's actually outperforming some of our veterans at ol' B&G. Shows initiative."

"Cute young thang too. That doesn't hurt."

"Haven't really noticed that, Glover. Too busy thinking about this sexy young thang in front of me."

"You always say the right things, Mr. Dunning."

6

Max

I was awakened from a very peaceful sleep when my McNeese State T-shirt landed on my bed. It was Valerie, the tall blonde from the Promenade in Santa Monica. She and her friend, Kaylen, were grad students from USC. Things went off *very* well with them the previous night. We all wound up back at my apartment that evening and they even waited while Smitty and I cleaned up. We ordered out from the local pizza joint and ordered a couple of pay-per-views.

Smitty was his usual crazy self and was the life of the party. He had us literally falling down laughing while we played cards and finished off a couple of bottles of my finest discount wine. Things started getting a little heavy between Valerie and me as the night went on. A kiss stolen here and there between laughs at first. To be honest, I was a little hesitant at first with the whole interracial thing. I had fooled around with some Chicanas and Filipinos since moving out here, but to me that was different. It was all brown skin! I had stuck to sisters strictly in Lake Charles as I felt more comfortable with that and there tended to be less "fraternization" there between whites and blacks.

As the little get-together started winding down, Valerie wound up wrapped around me and my reservations and misgivings faded. Kaylen with the ass for days had decided that Smitty wasn't going to be getting any of that ass and was ready to go home. I gave Smitty my keys to bring Kaylen home as

Valerie and I decided to get better acquainted. My supply of condoms came in handy that night as we trashed the bedroom. It was hot and passionate as we explored every inch of each other while catching our breath in between sessions.

"Hey, sleepy head! Mind if I use your shower?" Valerie was standing there buck-naked.

"Nah. I thought we used it last night." My exhausted ass was still trying to be smooth.

"McNeese, huh. In Lake Charles, right?" said Valerie as she pointed to the shirt she had just discarded.

"What do you know about Lake Charles?"

"I've got relatives from Alexandria. Isn't that near Lake Charles?"

"Damn. Small world."

"It's just L.A., Max. A town of transplants. Everybody winds up here. I guess you did too, huh?"

"Yeah."

"Care to join me in the shower? I have class today and have to run home first so I've got to get a move on." Her wink told me that she wanted her back scrubbed.

I was dead tired, but my ego was coming into play. This mandingo warrior wasn't about to show weakness. "Be right there."

After our shower interlude, I walked Valerie to her car, which was parked in front of my apartment's patio. We exchanged numbers and a couple of kisses before her Rav4 disappeared down Venice Boulevard toward the 405. I wondered deep down if either of us would be calling the other. Smitty didn't waste any time as his sliding glass door on the second floor came flying open.

"Awww! Somebody got some last night! No more handjobs huh, *Maxwell*?"

"Fuck you, Smit!"

"You could have left the door open last night, nigga! My cup on the floor didn't do the trick. You guys sounded like some mice down there all squeekin' and shit!"

"You are sick. You know that, right?"

"Damn straight! Sick from not getting laid last night. I hoped short-stuff would've changed her mind when I brought her home last night. Speaking of which . . . I've got your keys . . . and won't give them back until you come up here and give me details, fool!"

"I'm about to go up there and kick yo ass, *fool!*"

After getting my keys back from my unruly upstairs neighbor I decided to get some sleep. Smitty was going in to work at Home Stop this morning and I didn't go in to Denny's until tonight.

7
Glover

Lionel was waiting for me when I walked out of work that Tuesday. My Civic was still in the shop for warranty work on the transmission so I had been bumming a ride with Mona.

I was going to spend the evening with Lionel and he had called me earlier in the day to let me know that he was going to pick me up. Charmaine was grinning when she saw his Volvo on the parking lot and ran past Mona and me.

"Charmaine really needs to stop." Mona was staring at the cloud of smoke behind Charmaine as she beat a path to Lionel's car.

"You know how she is, Mona, always full steam ahead. That's why we love her."

"Sometimes I'd love to strangle her," said Mona with a chuckle.

Charmaine had made it to Lionel's window. Lionel lowered his window with a smile that revealed those pretty teeth.

"Hey Lionel!"

"Hello Charmaine! How are you?"

"Fine! Look at you, all spiffy and stuff! You know I'm mad at you, right?"

"What did I do?"

"You haven't hooked me up with one of your boys! What's up with that?!?"

"Well, most of my boys are already involved and . . . "

"Okay! Okay! I know! You just don't want this white girl to blow their minds and I understand. Really, I do. But enough of that . . . when's the big day? You can't keep my girl over there waiting and stuff." Good ol' Charmaine. Rapid fire as usual.

I figured that was my cue to save Lionel from Charmaine being Charmaine. I entered Lionel's car from the passenger side and gave him a quick kiss.

"Alright, Charmaine. Behave yourself." I was leaning over across Lionel's lap. Part of me was wondering what my motives were for saving Lionel from answering Charmaine's question. Was I avoiding the issue myself? Did I not want to hear the answer?

"Hey, Mona. How have you been?" said Lionel as Mona appeared over Charmaine's shoulder.

"I've been doing fine, Mr. Dunning," said Mona in her usual crisp tone. Her usual sophistication was showing through.

"Ms. McDaniel? Will you be needing a ride to work in the morning?" Mona was being messy in her own way and was wearing a dry smile.

Lionel's eyes then focused on me. He was waiting to see if I planned on spending the night with him or if I was going home as usual.

"I'll . . . I'll call you later, Mona." Lionel was smiling as well as Mona and Charmaine who looked like a pair of Cheshire cats.

"Bye guys!!! Y'all are too much." I felt like I was being ganged up on.

Lionel raised the window and we were off. Lionel had talk radio on in the Volvo as we headed for the Santa Monica Freeway from downtown. Traffic was heavy as everyone was pouring out of work at the same time onto all arteries leading from downtown L.A.

"Your friends are a wild bunch." Lionel was switching stations, as he knew I hated talk radio. "I don't think I'd get any work done with those two in my office. Haha."

"Yeah. They can carry on at times . . . especially Charmaine, but they take care of business too. But enough talk about work. Where are we gonna eat!" Lionel laughed as I kicked my shoes off and stretched. As I stretched, my skirt slid slightly up my leg. Lionel tried to play it off, but I saw his eyes locked on my thighs.

"Don't wreck," I said playfully. "It would take forever for a tow truck to come out in this traffic."

We exited I-10 at La Brea Avenue and made the trip north to my apartment on San Vicente. I had Lionel park his Volvo in my vacant parking spot in back since my car was in the shop. Lionel waited patiently in my living room while I changed into some warmups. Lionel took the time to loosen up and took off his tie and shirt. The sight of him in his slacks and undershirt was definitely appealing. We left for Lionel's house in the Hollywood Hills. We stayed off highway 101 to avoid the traffic. We took Cahuenga Boulevard north instead, stopping at Pasta To Go on the way. We ordered the shrimp fettuccini dinner with garlic bread and two small salads in the drive-thru. It took about thirty minutes to get from my apartment to Lionel's neighborhood, but what a difference.

Lionel stayed in an elegant Spanish-style home nestled in the neighborhoods off Franklin Ave. It was a three bedroom, two bath, walled spread with oak floors, a fireplace, and a humongous walk-in closet in Lionel's room. The closet itself made moving in with Lionel a very appealing proposal. Most of the homes were in the four hundred thousand plus range and Lionel's was no exception. Lionel was doing very well at his job and his parents' old L.A. money probably didn't hurt either with landing him this house.

We pulled in past the gate and under the carport. Lionel unloaded his papers, laptop, and briefcase from the car while I carried the dinner. I set the dinner at the kitchen table while Lionel put his things away. I found a bottle of 1995 Cabernet Sauvignon and a couple of wineglasses from the cabinet. Lionel came down the stairs and put some jazz on. The stereo system was wired into the house and the music came through the kitchen speaker.

"Aww! You set everything up! You are an angel." Lionel was wearing his college fraternity T-shirt and some shorts. He came into the kitchen and gave me a peck on the cheek.

"I am, aren't I? Ready to eat?"

"Yep."

Dinner went smoothly as we went over the day's happenings and unwound at the kitchen table. Lionel had some cookies and cream ice cream in the freezer and we shared a bowl for dessert.

We retired up to Lionel's bedroom with the remainder of the bottle of wine and decided to unwind further in his garden-sized bathtub. The jazz music followed us into the bathroom. I had left my clothes on the floor of Lionel's bedroom and stepped up into the bubbles. As I got comfortable, Lionel flipped the switch to turn on the whirlpool jets.

"Mmmmmmmm. That's good."

"Don't you think you should call Mona?" Lionel had just disrobed, allowing me a view of his tight, ebony physique before it disappeared into the tub.

"I'll call in a little bit. Besides . . . I don't know yet. I may go back home tonight."

"You know what I've been thinking about?" Lionel had a strange look on his face, but I couldn't tell if it was from the wine.

"No. What?"

"We haven't taken a trip in a while . . . and I was thinking. Do you feel like having fun?"

"Yes I feel like having fun. What are you getting at Lionel?"

"Oh . . . nothing. I'll let you know more next week."

"Next week!?!? What are you up to?"

"Be patient. You'll see . . . next week." At that point, Lionel leaned forward in the tub toward me. As Lionel's head descended into the bubbles and as my eyes began to roll back in my head, I began to think seriously about making that call to Mona.

8

Max

I slept through most of the day after Valerie left. The sleep was much needed. I was pulling a double shift at Denny's down on Hawthorne that evening. I turned the TV on to *Sportscenter* to see if there were any highlights from last night's Lakers' game and went to the kitchen to fix a quick snack of cold pizza. My pager on the counter was beeping. I probably had a couple of pages while I was sleeping.

"Yep, it was Jay." He was probably working at the mall tonight and was checking on my schedule. My cousin, Jay worked at the Male Tree men's store in the Del Amo Fashion Center Mall located right across the street from Denny's. We would hang out on our breaks and stuff. He was less than a year older than me, but looked out for me as if he was older. This was kinda out of character for him, as he hadn't been completely responsible with his own life. I guess Jay felt like he had to watch his country cousin's back in the big, bad land of L.A.

I found the phone in the bedroom. It was on the floor where it had fallen during last night's funfest with Valerie. Time to call Jay before he starts worrying.

The phone was ringing.

"Hello?"

"Hey, Uncle Maurice!"

"Max, that you boy?" Thirty plus years on the West Coast hadn't erased the Frenchman's accent of Uncle Mo. It was almost as if he had never left from "Down East".

"Yep, it's me. How are you doing?"

"Doing good, boy! Doing good! When you comin' by to eat? I know you don't be cookin' any home cooked meals in your apartment. Speakin' of that . . . you talk to your momma lately?" Uncle Mo loved to bombard you with multiple questions.

"I've been kinda busy so I haven't . . ."

"Well you need to call her. Hold on! I'm getting Maurice Jr. on the phone. *Junior*!!!"

I could hear Jay mumbling something when he took the phone from his dad. Jay was born Maurice J. Chavis Jr. but hated being compared to anyone hence his preference for "Jay".

"Whaddup, cuz."

"Whaddup, Jay. Sorry, but I just woke up a little while ago."

"It's alright. I was just checking to see if you workin' tonight. I gotta close tonight at the mall."

"Yeah. I'm working tonight. I'm getting ready to put this funky uniform on now. Samir's working tonight. He's pretty easy to work for so it should go smoothly tonight."

"I'll probably pass by Denny's on my way in. Any new women started workin' there?"

"No, cuz! Always tryin' to mack, huh?"

"You know me, cuz. Business . . . never personal."

I finished putting my uniform on and headed out the door. As I jumped in my Celica, I noticed the door had a new ding in it. The car was already starting to show its age. It didn't need the added help of my neighbors. I took I-405 south down to Hawthorne Boulevard. While I was stopped at the light on Rosecrans, I felt a little bass coming from the car on the side of me. It was this sister on the side of me in a green Volkswagen Cabriolet. She had her head nodding to the rap that was playing in her ride and smiled at me as I checked her out. I was admiring her as well as the rims on her ride. Both her and her ride had it going on. Brotherman thought he was about to get some digits when I realized that I had my damn Denny's uniform on.

"Shit," I whispered to myself. This was not good. She was lowering her radio to talk to me as I started scrunching down in my seat. The light turned green so I decided to cut my losses and took off. In my rearview mirror, I saw that she hadn't turned off and Denny's was just up ahead on my left. I turned into Denny's parking lot. I had pulled into my parking spot when I looked back and saw the Cabriolet stopped behind me just off the street.

"What am I doing? Am I some kind of worm? I'm a good-looking brother, there's a fine ass woman out there, and I'm sitting in here hiding out because of this uniform? I should be proud to have a damn job! I'm acting like a little kid when it's obvious that it doesn't matter what I'm wearing. Hell, I could be wearing a chicken suit . . . "

I was brimming with confidence when I stepped out of my car . . . .

That was until she saw my uniform. The last thing I heard was the chirp of her tires as she shifted gears and sped off down Hawthorne. Oh well. I guess she didn't want to hear about the discount that I could have given her on a grandslam breakfast. Her loss.

After throwing my hands up, I went on in to work and clocked in. It looked like business was light, which is something I liked. Samir was explaining something on the menu in his best dimestore Spanish to this elderly Mexican guy when I came out of the back.

Samir was the manager at Denny's and one of the nicest people I've ever known. He worked his way up since starting right out of high school. He was promoted to manager a couple of years back. It was right after the fallout from the discrimination lawsuits. Samir was a heavyset brother with a gold tooth. He was married with three kids, one of which was his own, and lived in Gardena. You always knew where you stood with him and he was never one to bullshit you. Samir was all about helping brothers get ahead and I was lucky to have him as my manager.

"Glad you could make it, Max!" Samir had looked up from the menu he was explaining to acknowledge me.

"Thanks, Samir."

There were a few tables that needed cleaning, so I got started on them. I did a little bit of everything when I worked this shift, be it cleaning tables or waiting on customers.

When I was on my third table, I noticed Jay's red BMW 328 glistening there on the parking lot. Jay always kept it clean, as it was his pride and joy. Just then Jay strolled in the door. He had on his shirt and tie with a pair of black slacks. His typical work attire.

"You missed a plate, Country!" Jay loved to rib me even though he couldn't take it when he was on the receiving end.

"Nah. I left that one for you. You might need the crumbs for some of those little crumb snatchers around town that you don't claim." I made that up, but figured it would bother him.

"Awww. You know that ain't me. Just like Michael Jackson said, "The kid is not my son." Besides . . . I know better than to fall into that trap."

Jay was Mr. Ladies' Man. He was twenty-six and had the style, the looks, and the car. Most of our family was Creole and the "Good Hair Fairy" had waved its wand over Jay giving him the straight black shit on his head. Due to the hair issue, he also had a lot of sisters wanting to have his baby out here. For all Jay had going for him, he was still drifting through life. Jay still lived with his parents, worked in the mall, and dropped out of college after a few years over at UCLA. Hell, Uncle Mo bought him the Bimmer just before he dropped out.

"Hey Jay, do you ever think about going back to school?"

"What made you bring that up, cuz?"

"I don't know. I was just thinking."

"I might . . . one day. I just need to be ready up *here* when I do." said Jay while pointing at his head. Jay seemed to be a thousand miles away before he caught himself.

"I hear ya, cuz. Well, I've got work to do. Samir's cool, but he does expect me to work some of the time!"

"Yeah. I've gotta get over to M. Tree and make those sales. Oh! Before I forget . . . Pops want to you to come over for dinner later this week. You are lookin' a little poor."

"How about this Friday?"

"Alright. I'll holler at you later."

9

Glover

I finally got my Civic out of the shop so I made plans to hang with Mona Friday night. We decided to lounge at her crib down on Ocean Avenue in Santa Monica. Lord knows Mona's view was better than mine. I picked up D'Angelo's new CD on my way there and was scanning through the tracks as I pulled into Mona's parking lot. The sun was setting over the Pacific as the waves rolled in down on the beach. I stayed in the doorway of my car for a couple of seconds to take in the view. California. It doesn't get any better.

I walked into the colorful lobby past the doorman. He had seen me before so no questions were asked, just a simple smile and hello. I saw that they had changed the plants in front as I waited for the elevator. The elevator opened and I entered. I gave the doorman a parting smile as I pushed the number seven button and ascended to Mona's crib.

When I arrived outside Mona's door, I could hear the same D'Angelo CD playing. I guess we were more like sisters than I thought. I let out a giggle as I rang the doorbell. Mona answered the door and was probably wondering what was so funny. Mona was wearing her usual home apparel, a long T-shirt (this one had her dad's real estate company logo on it) and a pair of black stretch pants. What really surprised me was the do-rag tied around Mona's head, which came to a knot in the front. Mona almost *never* let anyone catch her with a rag, hairnet, etc. on her head. Actually, anyone who's ever been by Mona's house has never seen her out of her "diva-wear". If you hadn't kicked it with her like I had, it was kind of hard to believe that Mona had a tomboy side to her.

I couldn't let the do-rag thing go so I said, "What's up, Tupac?"

"You are the funny one, Ms. McDaniel." Mona couldn't help but laugh at herself.

"You better duck back in before your neighbors see."

"Oh, they've seen me like this before."

"When? Last time the building caught on fire?"

"Get in here!"

Mona yanked me in through the door causing me to almost trip over my own feet.

"I see you got that new D'Angelo too, huh? I just picked mine up on the way here, matter of fact."

"Yeah. Well, actually Craig bought it for me. He left it with my doorman downstairs. He also bought those flowers on the counter over there. He's still trying, but I'm not feeling him. I do appreciate the CD though . . . and the flowers do smell good!"

I scooted across the carpet and walked over to Mona's counter to get a closer look at the flowers. They were a beautiful splash of colors—purple, yellow, and pink. The card that came with them was lying there, but I didn't want to be nosey . . . yet.

"Awww! They're beautiful! I think it's really sweet of him to do this for you. Are you sure about dumping him? You guys do make a cute couple." I was giving Mona the guilty look.

"Yeah. I'm sure. Besides, we were never *really* a couple. I made that very clear to him."

Craig was Mona's most recent paramour/conquest. They met about six months ago. The brother was 6'5 inches of solid man who happened to be a trainer at Body Systems USA. Mona had a trial membership to Body Systems, which was actually a gift from this dude named Rico. Well, Mona strolls on into the gym in one of her cute little designer workout sets and runs smack into Craig. I wondered if she was going to have the nerve to keep going there after this all played out.

"Are you ever going to settle down, girl? I thought you might do that with that Brazilian dude a while back." I had plopped down on her couch and was thumbing through one of Mona's *Essence* magazines.

"Who? You mean Romi? I wasn't about to move back to Sao Paulo with him. I was fond of him though. Besides, we all can't have someone like Lionel. Now, can we?" Mona was getting tired of the sermon and decided to turn the tables.

"Okay. Touché. What are we getting into tonight? Let's move on to another subject other than men."

"Alright. You hungry? I've got some leftovers in the fridge."

"Nah. I picked up a burger on the way home from work. Did you get your hair done?"

"Yeah, girl. I was overdue for a relaxer. Naps were starting to show. I headed straight for Inglewood after work! Can you believe that I actually got out of there at a decent time? Speaking of decent . . . when are you going to let me do those crusty nails of yours?"

"Haha. Fuck you, bitch! For your information, they are not crusty . . . but feel free to give me that manicure, girl!" Mona was da bomb when it came to manicures. She even had her own little kit. She could probably do a mean pedicure, but Ms. Mona wasn't about to go near the sister's toes.

We spent the rest of the night reminiscing and yakking it up. D'Angelo was playing, we talked about this book we both read, Mona tightened my nails up and all was well in the world. The subject eventually returned to men, of course.

"Lionel has something up his sleeve for next week, but I don't know what." I was actually thinking out loud.

"You think he's going to pop the question?"

"I don't know, Mona. To be perfectly honest . . . I'm not sure if that's what I want." I can't believe I finally admitted that. Mona's mouth dropped to the carpet, but she tried to play it off.

"Girl, you know I'm *never* sure about anything like that. Sounds like you've got a lot of thinking to do."

"Yeah. You're right. I just want to be certain that it's real for me if it comes to that. God, I wish my mom was here. I miss her so much." I had started crying and didn't realize it until Mona reached over and handed me a tissue. She then gave me a long hug.

"Mona, you know what would be good now?"

"No. What?" Mona didn't know where I was going with this.

"Ice cream. Lots of it. My mom used to fix me ice cream and it would make everything better. Is Bracken's still open at this time of night?" Even with my droopy red eyes, I managed to crack a smile.

"Girl! You know damn well I'm not going out looking like th . . . *Sigh*. Let me get a hat or something." Yep. Mona was a true friend.

10

Max

I was finally on my way down to Uncle Maurice and Aunt Verna's house for dinner that Friday night. Uncle Mo was a retired shop foreman and was enjoying the good life now. They had been living in the same two-story house in Carson for twenty-plus years. Uncle Mo had the means to move out to the suburbs, but he chose to stay where his heart was. Uncle Mo had a certain pride about him and refused to let any trends dictate his life. He had been through everything from the Watts Riots to the L.A. uprising and wasn't budging.

My mom told me how Uncle Mo and Aunt Verna hooked up. Uncle Mo had just moved to L.A. and was living in Compton when he first met Aunt Verna. Aunt Verna was an Opelousas, Louisiana native and they met at one of those Zydeco dances or "la-las" popular with the Creoles residing in southern California. They fell in love and were shortly married. Uncle Mo was working as a longshoreman back then.

When I arrived at Uncle Mo's, I saw his new gold Caddy in the driveway next to Jay's Bimmer. The big Deville was Uncle Mo's treat to himself and it came with all the bells and whistles. I parked along the curb, as the driveway was full. As I approached the door, the wind carried the smell of mustard greens my way. Aunt Verna was throwing down. This was going to be good. *Real good.*

Fried chicken, mustard greens with salt pork, turnips, potato salad, and buttered rolls. High blood pressure heaven! I loved dinners at Uncle Mo's. I don't know why I didn't come over more often for this. Jay, Uncle Mo, and I were sitting around getting our grub on at the table, as Aunt Verna was finishing up in the kitchen. She was always the last one to the table, as she never wanted a hand with the cooking. If Uncle Mo's home was his castle, then the kitchen was Aunt Verna's own little private tower.

"You need to bring your ass here more often, Country. We normally don't eat this good." Jay was pulling a roll apart as he leaned over and whispered in my ear.

"You need to cut that 'Country' shit out. Your southern California ass has more of a twang than I do, *Junior*." I was enjoying the food too much to put up with Jay's shit.

"F..fff..fuck you. Country ass nigga." No one outside the family knew that Jay used to have a really bad stutter as a child. It was under control now, but if you knew what buttons to push it would come flying back.

Uncle Mo had just killed a chicken leg and was glancing over at Jay and me. I knew what was coming.

"Maxwell, you call your momma yet, boy? She called here the other day. Her and your Auntie Verna talked for a little bit. That lady there. She miss her boy."

"No sir. I haven't called her yet. I will be calling her *this* weekend. I promise." I was starting to feel bad.

"Yeah, baby. You know she already think somethin' gonna happen to you out here," Aunt Verna chimed in as she sat down at the table.

"How's your job search comin' along, boy? You and your little neighbor still lookin'?" Uncle Mo didn't particularly like Smitty as he thought he was odd.

"Yes, sir. We're both still looking. We're planning on going downtown next week. The Business District, employment office, and all that. I'm hoping to land something soon. I thought it would be a little easier when I first decided to move out here."

"Well, son. The economy's good, but there's so much competition out there. You need to convince your cousin Junior to finish school and try to get a good payin' job too. That boy there. He spend too much time chasin' them women when he needs to be takin' care of business." Uncle Mo spoiled Jay to some extent, but he wasn't a pushover. He didn't plan on taking care of Jay his entire life.

"Aww, Pops!" Jay excused himself from the table and went upstairs to his room.

Damn. Here I was really looking forward to dessert, but the looks from Uncle Mo and Aunt Verna were urging me on to go talk to Jay. I guess I could get some dessert with my take-home plate. I excused myself from the table and strolled up the stairs to Jay's door.

I shouted through Jay's door, "You know I'm missing dessert, right?" I noticed the door was partially open and walked in. Jay was lying across his bed while looking up at the ceiling. Yep. He was pissed. He had his DMX playing on his stereo.

"You alright, cuz?"

"Yeah. They didn't need to send you up here. I'm not some damn kid. Fool's always on my case."

"You know he loves you though. They both do."

"Yeah. I know. That's why I'm gonna do them a favor and move the hell out soon. Maybe move in with one of these chickenheads for awhile." Jay was pointing up at the various pictures on his wall of some of his "lady friends". The pictures ranged from model poses to bikini shots and they all looked *damn* good. I kinda wondered what kinds of personalities these "Jet Beauties of the Week" had to go along with their looks.

"You know you're welcome to move in with me, cuz."

"Thanks, man. I'll think about that. I think I'm gonna crash now if you don't mind."

"Nah. Not at all. Talk to you later, cuz."

"Yeah. I'll probably pay you a visit at the apartment tomorrow."

And with that, I was dismissed.

11 *Glover*

Saturday night rolled around and it was time for the three amigas to hit the town. There was this new club on the Strip called Drama that we wanted to check out. The name was certainly appropriate for this town where everyone was either an actor between gigs or an aspiring actor. We just hoped there would be no drama when we arrived there.

Charmaine, who lived in the Valley, drove down to Mona's where she left her car. Mona had more room in her 626, so we were rolling with her this night. Charmaine grew up around Crenshaw and moved to the Valley with her family while she was still in high school. Even though Charmaine still lived there, my white sister was more L.A. than Valley.

I was toweling myself dry after showering when I heard the cackling outside the door. It was time for the sisters to get rowdy. I wrapped myself up and let them in.

"Hey now! It's time to paaaaaaaaaaaarrrrrrrrrrty," Charmaine yelled as she danced on in the door. I could tell that she had started celebrating earlier in the day. Mona walked in behind Charmaine with a simple "Hey.".

"Hey, y'all. Make yourselves comfortable. I'll be ready in a minute."

"Bitch, *please*. Your ass is gonna take more than a minute." Charmaine always had a lovely way of putting things. She was right though.

I looked back over my shoulder and gave Charmaine a mischievous grin. That was right before I yanked the wet towel from around me and threw it in right in Charmaine's face. Charmaine was still spitting as I slowly strolled my naked ass into my bedroom.

I was in my room transforming myself for the night. While looking in the mirror, I made mental note to get my highlights redone soon. Mona had sat down on my sofa and was looking through my photo album while Charmaine was thumbing through my CDs. I put my hair up and went with my femme fatale attire: the black silk halter-top and black jeans topped off with the black Jones of New York jacket. Mona was going with some china-doll routine that only she could pull off: a very tight fitting collared, blue sleeveless dress with splashes of red in it. Mona accessorized it with gold bracelets on both arms. Charmaine went with the black as I did. She had a short black skirt with splits on both sides, which was topped off with a black sleeveless blouse. Charmaine had her reddish-brown hair teased.

It was ladies night at Club Drama so we got in free. The men were paying that night, so they were out to recoup their fifteen dollars in either phone numbers or something with a little more substance. Charmaine would probably refer to that something as "ass". Drama used to be a techno club and I had been here once back then. It was interesting to see how different management would put its stamp on this former print shop and change its appearance every time. Drama promised to have a hip hop/dance feel, but for a mature set and it appeared to be delivering. Charmaine and I were nodding our heads as we strolled through the joint. Mona was in diva mode so her head-nodding would be limited this night.

There were truly some good looking brothers in the place trying to get their mack on. I was involved so I would simply smile politely and turn down their requests for the digits.

Charmaine was out on the dance floor making a scene with this brother who had his hair dyed blonde . . . must be an athlete. Mona was working the place as she glided around. This was Mona doing her thing. All eyes on her. Brothers were turning away from their dates to sneak a peek when Ms. Thang was nearby. It was a bold confidence Mona had about herself in this environment that would have most women calling her a bitch. I have to admit that I would probably be right there with them if I didn't really know Mona or if I was insecure about myself.

"Oooo. Your eyes." I was snapped out of my club watching by this light brown-skinned brother with an electric-blue suit. He was standing on the side of me and smiling.

With a bewildered look, I said, "Huh?"

"Your eyes. I just noticed. What are they? Hazel?" He apparently had been staring at me for a while.

"Yep, hazel. You got it. What's your name?" I figured it was best to take control of this situation. It usually caught a brother off guard.

"Umm . . . Terry. I'm from Cleveland. You ever been there?"

"Nope. Never been there, Terry. What brings you here?"

"I'm in town for a television producers convention. Staying at the Doubletree downtown. Heading back tomorrow. You never did tell me your name." He was so busy trying to remember his lines that he almost forgot to ask my name.

"Glover." My drink was getting all watery on me. Time for another one.

"That's an interesting name. Can I buy you another drink, Glover?"

"Nah. I'm not drinking another one."

Terry continued talking, but something else had my attention. Craig was in the club.

Craig had spotted Mona and had skirted around the edge of the dance floor to get to where Mona was standing. Of course, Mona was in the company of someone else at that moment. Craig didn't look too happy and interrupted Mona's conversation. Mona excused the startled young gentleman as her and Craig were getting into a heated discussion. The heat appeared to be one sided as Craig was pointing and flailing his arms about as Mona stood there unemotional, arms folded, with one of her eyebrows raised.

"Umm. Terry? I'm seeing someone so you may wish to try to hook up with someone else tonight. Okay?"

Charmaine had noticed Mona's situation from the dance floor and was walking toward me. Terry stood there dumbfounded for a second then walked off. I'm sure I heard the word "bitch" as he disappeared into the crowd. He was kinda cute though.

"G-love. You see that shit? Craig's going off on Mona over there."

"Let's get over there before something stupid happens."

Charmaine and I began moving through the crowd toward their location. As we got closer, the music was still too loud to hear what was being said. Just as we closed in on them, Craig raised his hand as if to hit Mona then suddenly dropped his massive arm and stormed off.

Charmaine asked, "You okay, Mona?" with a look of relief on her face.

"Yes. I am fine. It's Craig that's not. I guess he finally understands what 'over' means." Mona had her ice queen face on. The entire incident really didn't seem to phase her.

I asked, "I guess you're ready to go, huh?"

Then Mona surprised me.

"No. Why? The night is still young. Craig is the least of my concerns." Mona said it in her dry manner. The diva rolled on . . . for a little while longer.

Mona had just started to walk off to continue her rounds when Craig returned. His little walk didn't cool him off, as he still looked pissed.

In the middle of the club with everybody looking, Craig stopped in front of Mona and screamed at her, "*You lousy bitch*!!!" then walked off. I guess he reconciled himself to doing that instead of hitting Mona. A hush fell over the ground level of the club. I could almost hear the music pause in the place. *Now* it was time to leave.

On the drive home, Mona didn't say a word. Craig had actually succeeded in embarrassing her I guess. She would be over it by tomorrow. Charmaine was pissed off because she couldn't find the blonde brother after Mona's scene and lost that phone number. So much for there not being drama at Club Drama.

12 *Max*

I woke up early Sunday morning and decided to do some major cleaning. My funky clothes needed to be washed, my car was too dirty, and the apartment was a mess. I straightened things out around the place first then decided to tackle the wash. On the way down to the laundry room, I saw Smitty hanging out near the pool. Gawking at Mrs. Barnes, no doubt. Couldn't fault him. For an older lady, she was fine as hell . . . and her swim wear didn't leave much to the imagination. I convinced Smitty to hang out with me later as I washed my car on the parking lot. He decided to wash his hooptie too, as his car was running today. But first, I needed to call my mom.

Adding two hours to the time due to the Central Time zone, I figured my mom would be back home. Orelia always went to the early mass at St. Henry's, then hung out and chatted with the other parishioners. It was like clockwork unless there was a church barbecue or fair. If that was the case, Orelia could be out for several hours. I decided to take the chance there was no fair.

"Hello?"

"Hey, mom! "

"Max! How's my baby doing?" I would always be her baby, even when old and gray. I had given up on trying to stop her from referring to me by that.

"I'm fine, mom. You just got back from mass?"

"Yeah, baby. I saw Ms. Duplechein in church today. Remember her? She used to do the sewing for us. Anyway, she asked how you were doing. I told her you were in California."

"Yeah, mom. Her son still in jail?"

"I think so, baby. She don't talk much about him, so I don't ask. You know your cousin, Huey died? You never met him, but I know I mentioned him before. Well, he had a heart attack just last week. I went to the wake."

"No. I don't remember him. How are you doing, mom? Uncle Maurice said he spoke with you."

" I'm doin' fine, baby. Just the old arthritis every now and then. I hadn't heard from you, but I didn't want to be a bother. How's your money lookin'?"

"I'm okay. I just need to find a permanent job soon. Me and my neighbor are going downtown this week. I hear the state's hiring."

"Ooo. Downtown. Just be careful down there. I heard they have some winos that try to mess with people." I had to snicker. Mom had a habit of excessive worrying at times.

"No problem, mom! I'll be on the lookout when I go down there."

"Did you enjoy dinner at your Uncle's? I know Verna can put too much salt in her food sometimes." Uh oh. The old competitiveness flaring up.

"Oh, it was fine, mom! . . . well, it was good . . . just not as good as your cooking." There. That should make her feel better.

"Oh, you're so sweet! That's why I'm gonna fix you a big ol' meal when you come home!"

"Aww. Thanks, mom. It may be a while though. I'm planning on making a go of it out here. Once I get permanently situated, I'll probably be able to fly down . . . to visit."

"Just don't be showin' up with any of them wild California women on your arm. You need to get a good girl from right down here, not one of them siddity little wenches." Uh oh. Time to go.

"Mom, you need to stop. Haha! Lake Charles has plenty of its own wild women . . . and some siddity ones too!" Besides, I hadn't found the right woman for me anywhere yet.

37

"Well, I guess you got a point there."

"Mom?"

"Yeah, baby?"

"I love you."

"I love you too, baby!"

After talking with my mom, I went outside to wash the ride. Smitty was already out there with his bucket and soap. He had a confused look on his face as he looked at his hooptie.

Smitty said, "You know, dawg . . . I'm a little afraid to wash the ride. The dirt might be all that's holding it together."

"That's not it. You're just lazy out here. Don't want to get your hands dirty and shit."

"Hey. I get my damn hands dirty enough when I'm at work at Home Stop. These hands are for the ladies, dawg. Y'see, I've got my priorities straight!"

"Whatever, Smit."

Smitty eventually got around to cleaning the hooptie. We watched the neighbors come and go while doing a little detailing and stuff on the rides. I was spraying tire shine when the familiar red BMW pulled up and parked behind my Celica.

"Uh oh. Cousin Junior's in da house!" Smitty yelled out when he saw Jay's car.

"Shhhh! Call him 'Jay', Smitty," I hissed back. I regret that day I told him about the "Junior" issue.

Jay finished listening to whatever song was on the radio, then got out of his car.

Jay hollered, "Whaddup fellas?" as he walked toward us. He was wearing one of the new Lakers jerseys and a pair of navy denim shorts with his shades pulled up on his head. He looked a little rough around the edges. Probably from partying the night before.

I responded back, "Whaddup, cuz?" Smitty gave Jay a nod.

"Gettin' it clean, cuz? You can do mine next." Jay's ride was already spotless.

"I'll clean that Bimmer for you, Jay," said Smitty, while cheesin',"if you leave it with me for the day. Whatchasay?"

"I say yo little skinny ass better look, smell, and talk like Nia Long before I would even consider that. Last time I looked, you couldn't even come close to that. Not even if you had one of them surgeries to cut your little nuts and wee wee off! Ha!"

Smitty didn't find Jay's comments that funny. Me? I was laughing. I couldn't believe he said, "wee wee".

"Went out last night, huh Jay?"

"Yeah, cuz. That's why I wasn't able to roll by yesterday. I was all over town hunting up a new suit. Let a true player fill you wannabes in on what went down last night!"

13 *Glover*

It was Tuesday at work before Mona had loosened up again. Charmaine and I had exchanged whispers here and there since the drama at Drama, but we were still avoiding the subject when in Mona's presence. Lionel called me before lunch that day. He wanted me to meet him at his office down on Grand Avenue in the CBD, as he needed to discuss something with me. Normally, we would meet up somewhere for lunch due to my short lunch hour. Perhaps Lionel would have lunch waiting for me this time.

As I drove down Grand Avenue toward Lionel's office in the Gas Company Tower, I was thinking about the changes the area had been through. The homeless had all but disappeared as they were "relocated" to other parts of downtown by design. That left the area more palatable for business. I watched as the professionals were milling about on their cell phones as they crossed the streets and overhead walkways and drove off to lunch in their Range Rovers and Volvo wagons. Thank God Lionel didn't have a wagon. Of course, if we did wind up marrying, a wagon might come in handy.

I pulled into the parking garage adjacent to the Tower and took the elevator up to the thirtieth floor where Barnes & Greenwood was headquartered. Lionel hooked up with them straight out of Stanford and had made a name for himself in just a few short years. For being one of the few brothers there, Lionel was considered a real "team player" and a trusted confidant. I wondered at times if the outcome would have been any different if Lionel didn't have the Dunning name to back him up. Probably not.

The lobby was bustling as usual with the suits, older white males in dark blue suits with red ties. Man, even Al Gore learned to change. At least Lionel didn't fall into that trap. My baby was stylish! I made my way over to the receptionist desk. I was about to ask for her to call Lionel, but I saw his office door was open. I had been there before and the office wasn't too stuffy to keep me from seeing my man. I was close enough to Lionel's office to read his nameplate when I was almost knocked off my feet. It was that eager-beaver chick, whatsherface. She flew out of Lionel's office like a bat outta hell and smack dab into me. She didn't look too happy either.

"Hi. Misha, right?" God, I hoped I was right with the name. I extended my hand. That's me, Ms. Courteous.

"Yes! How are you doing, Glover? Lionel's in his office. Sorry about almost bowling you over." Almost?

"That's okay!" Bitch. At least she knew my name.

"Well, I've got to run. Lunchtime. Nice seeing you again!" And with that Misha hustled out the office. She appeared to have returned to her normal perkiness.

I stepped into Lionel's office to see my baby standing there by his window. He was wearing the tie and suspender set I'd bought him last Christmas.

"Well hello, sir. Hope I didn't interrupt anything. Your friend almost ran over me on her way out."

"Nah, baby! Misha was pissed with her salary review and was telling me about it. She can be high-strung at times," said Lionel with those pearly whites glistening.

"*Oh really?* I didn't know she would confide in you like that, Mr. Dunning. Am I gonna have to keep an eye on her?" I gave Lionel my fake jealous face.

"Not at all, Ms. McDaniel. Come here, girl," said Lionel as he outstretched his arms. I walked over to plant a big kiss on him, but he cut the kiss short.

"Hey! What's up with that."

"The door's open, baby. I don't want anyone around here tripping . . . that's all."

"Well, I guess they would trip if I did this . . . " With that said, I discretely passed my hand between Lionel's legs and brushed against his manhood. Lionel jerked suddenly and protested a little, but figured no one could tell that we were doing anything else but hugging. As I felt Lionel harden, I stopped suddenly. I liked showing him who was boss at times and didn't like my kiss being cut short.

I looked up into Lionel's eyes and said, "I hope you had lunch delivered because I used most of my lunch time trying to park and make it up here."

"Well, I didn't have anything delivered except for what's on my desk there," replied Lionel as he pointed down.

On Lionel's desk were airline tickets as well as brochures. I saw the words "Orlando", "Disney", "Resort" and went crazy.

"Ooooooooohhhhhhhh Lionel!! Are we going somewhere? Is this the secret you mentioned the other night?"

"Yeah. You like?"

"Do I *like*? Oh, I like! Umm, when are you planning this for?"

"This weekend. We fly out of LAX this Friday and come back Monday evening."

"Monday? But I have to work Monday."

"Well, I guess you need to go back to that little office and tell them you need Monday off, huh? Or you could just quit . . . "

"Nope. Nice try. I'll take Monday off!"

"Good. Now we'll have some time to ourselves down in Orlando. No distractions, just rest and relaxation and time to talk about 'us'."

That last comment bothered me slightly, as I knew what that talk about "us" meant. I don't know why I was behaving like this, but I needed to start acting my age.

" I guess I need to do some shopping before Friday, huh?" I then grabbed Lionel and held him tightly in my arms.

14   *Max*

Friday had rolled around and the brothers all had a little change in their pocket. We couldn't think of any better way of relieving the stress than to do a little partying. Earlier in the day, I gave Smitty a ride to Home Stop to pick up his paycheck, then he rode with me down to Torrance to pick up my check from Denny's. Jay was at work in the mall at the time, so we paid him a visit too. Jay was to roll by the apartment after work that evening.

I was dancing around my living room in my draws with an iron in my hand. Al Green's "Love and Happiness" was taking me there as I ironed my midnight blue pullover shirt. I had showered and my Nautica was just right. I wanted the ladies to smell it, but I didn't want them choking off the fumes. Smitty had tightened the brother's "do" earlier, as my edges were a little rough and all I had to do now was pick it out a little. Jay was selecting our destination, as he actually volunteered to drive tonight. That was rare. We usually went in separate cars to give Jay the freedom to break out and get his "whap-whap". Humph, Jay probably needed to use the apartment tonight.

Jay arrived bearing gifts, Heineken. Lots of it. We had all agreed to go playa-casual for the night, so no suits. I threw on my shirt with some white linen slacks and my black troopers. Jay went the denim shirt route with the khakis. We hauled the Heineken upstairs to Smitty's and banged on his door. Smitty had the boomin' system so that would be our departure point. Smitty went "true playa" on us and was wearing one of his busy silk shirts with some black slacks and Stacys. So much for the stealth mode. I guess it was for the best that the *womens* knew we were coming from a block away. It gave them time to prepare.

We killed the Heinekens while telling the traditional stories of the women we'd had and of the ones we hoped to get tonight. Smitty had the walls shaking with DMX and Dr. Dre, but I hadn't heard any Cash Money in a while. I stumbled down the stairs to get a couple of their CDs and Smitty let me play them. Jay couldn't help but come with the "Country" shit at that point. It didn't bother me though because I had my buzz on, I was looking good, and I was in L.A.

Jay let us in on the destination once we were rolling. We were on our way to hang with the beautiful people at Captains in West Hollywood. Normally we had a slim chance of getting in the joint on a Friday night, but Jay went to high school with the brother at the door. That made our chances a *lot* better . . . well, that and twenty bucks. Jay never said they were really good friends in high school.

The beautiful people were in the house that night and the food was damn good too. I didn't need anything weighing me down so I had some gumbo in the dining room. It was pretty good. Not as good as home, but not that watery stuff that some places called "gumbo" out here. Smitty was going to town on some fried chicken like the fool hadn't eaten in days. Jay had moved on to the lounge and the ladies. We would be joining my cuz soon.

"Ay Max, that's all you're eatin' tonight?" said Smitty as he sucked on a chicken bone.

"Yeah, dawg. I don't want the bloated feeling tonight. Gotta stay light on my feet. Don't want to be belching around Tyra Banks, y'know?"

"I guess you got a point there. You ready to circulate?"

"Yeah. Let's do this!"

We decided to split up to cover more area. Smitty headed toward the bar while I went on into the crowded lounge. I spotted Jay in the corner. He was sitting on a barstool and had an audience of not one, but two women. One of the sisters was wearing this tight, backless light blue dress and had a cappuccino complexion with some pretty little braids going down her back. The other one had one of those cute permy-fros to go with her golden-tanned self and red dress. I could tell the two shopped together for their dresses.

I was about to slip by when Jay spotted me and motioned me over.

"Hey, cuz," Jay said while brimming with confidence, "I want you to meet my two friends here. Diane and Brandi, this is my cousin, Maxwell. Maxwell, these are my friends, Diane and Brandi." I could tell Jay was pulling some scam when he called me by my full name. Diane, in the blue dress, shook my hand and then slowly let go. There was eye contact as our hands parted that told me Diane was looking forward to spending a lot more time with me that evening. I could see her nipples popping up through her form-fitting dress and the thought of more time with Diane seemed *very* appealing. The brief conversation went well, until Jay told me to take a walk with him to the bar.

"Cuz, they are ready! I need to fill you in though. They think we're in the NFL. I told them we both play cornerback and come back to L.A. when our season ends."

"What!!?? Awww man! Why do you have to make up shit? You don't think people fall for that shit, do ya?"

"All the time, cuz. All the time. This is L.A., nigga! Everybody lies! Yo country ass is a fool if you haven't learned that yet. You need to wake up." Jay's smooth demeanor had faded temporarily. I paused to look back toward Diane and Brandi who were still smiling and waiting for us. I envisioned Diane riding me all night as I went up to the bar with Jay.

"After these drinks, we're outta here. I might even let Brandi drive the ride. Yeah. Then she can drive the *real* ride," said Jay with a prideful sneer.

"Wait! What about Smitty?" My lust had made me forget Smit for a second.

"Fuck him. Besides, there's not enough room in the ride for all of us. His runt ass can catch a cab with his bad shirt. I've got Pops' credit card, so it's time to get that room!"

"Aww, man. That's foul." This was one of those times I didn't like my cousin. I looked around our vicinity, but didn't see Smit. This was wrong.

We walked back to Diane and Brandi with their drinks and continued our talk with the ladies. I talked, but didn't contribute to Jay's lie. While I was looking around, Diane took a sip of her drink and pulled me into her. She began kissing me and opened her mouth to share her tongue as well as some of her drink. Our tongues locked up, as the taste of sweet rum went down my throat. Next thing I knew, the four of us were heading out of Captains and straight for Jay's Bimmer, which was parked across the street. Jay had his arm around a giggling Brandi, while Diane was skipping toward the car with me willingly in tow. Jay turned his alarm off and the doors unlocked. He appeared to be serious about letting Brandi drive. Everyone started entering the car and I was looking at Diane's ass as she bent over to enter. I couldn't dog my boy like that . . . or put up with Jay's lying ass anymore tonight.

"Hey! I just remembered. I gotta run back in the club. My agent's in there and we gotta . . . talk about my new deal." Weak. Real weak. "I'll catch up with you guys later."

The car erupted in a series of groans and gasps and I could read Jay's lips as "punk ass . . . " came out silently. Diane got out of the car and tried to convince me to leave with them. I let Jay keep his story and apologized to Diane before the three of them drove off down La Cienaga. Diane did give me one last long, wet kiss and placed my hands on her ass in an attempt to sway me. It almost worked. Almost. I did get her number though. Now, I not only had to locate Smitty and try to explain why we had to cab it home, but I had to figure out how to be let back inside Captains. Looking at the crowd outside now, I knew it would take more than a twenty to get back in there. *Sigh.* I could smell Diane's perfume all over my shirt.

15 *Glover*

Florida! The sunshine and palm trees, but without the smog. The flight was quiet and uneventful and allowed me and Lionel to get a little nap in. The rush to get to LAX on time had both of us worn out so we took advantage of the downtime in the air. The rental car was waiting for us upon touchdown in Orlando, which was no surprise as Lionel was always organized. I brought my camera, but didn't have any film yet. I was content to take in the view and commit it to memory as we drove down the tollway into town. Orlando had splashes of tropical colors everywhere on the buildings, etc. and little bodies of water here and there. Touristy, but still well manicured.

I had been to our amusement parks in Cali and had seen pictures of Orlando, but neither had prepared me for the beauty or sheer size of the actual attractions. We followed the directional signs, slowing to look at the map again, and eventually made it to our resort near Disney. Lionel's parents owned a time-share there. The place was humongous and I was feeling like a little kid as I stared up at all the levels above from the lobby. The staff was so courteous and friendly and brought our luggage up to the room after check-in. Lionel tipped them generously. This was going to be a fairy tale weekend.

I was feeling like a little girl all the way up to our room, but once the door was closed and locked that was over. It was time for Lionel to make me feel like a woman. I gave Lionel a devilish look and he responded immediately by pressing me against the door. I had nowhere to move and gripped the door handle tightly, nervously. Lionel's body pressed up against my pelvic region and I could feel him growing. My grip on the door handle tightened, while his tongue slid up and down my neck and across my ear. Lionel stopped by my ear to whisper some obscenities that he knew would drive me crazy. My legs started quivering, causing me to buck uncontrollably against the door as I pushed back against Lionel. Lionel paused to throw off his shirt then began to fondle my breasts in his hands. Lionel then reached up under my T-shirt and proceeded to undo my bra. I had released the door handle and was now reaching down to undo Lionel's belt. His shorts dropped to the floor revealing no underwear. My turn.

I caught Lionel off guard and pushed him back onto the king-size bed. I threw my shirt off and fell on top of Lionel's sleek, hard body. Lionel's left hand had found it's way between my thighs and was rubbing intensely while he used his right hand to hold one of my breasts. This allowed him to run his tongue across my nipple and to drive me even more into an uncontrolled frenzy. My shorts found their way onto the floor as well as my thong shortly after that. Lionel had rolled me onto my back and teased me for a while before entering inside me. By the time he entered, I was more than ready to take in all he had to give.

Needless to say, we wound up staying in the room the rest of the day and wound up ordering room service that night. The lovin' continued throughout the night with hardly any words spoken except for our animal grunts and growls.

Saturday morning arrived with a shock. We didn't get a chance to put the "Do Not Disturb" sign out, so room service had a surprise when the lady opened the door and caught us *au natural* across the bed. We were awakened right as she entered the room. I shrieked and grabbed the sheets, the lady shrieked as she turned her head and apologized in Spanish, and Lionel simply grunted and wondered what the hell was going on. After that start, the rest of the day was less of a roller coaster. Lionel and I took in the sights and walked for miles. Lionel even bought me some film for my camera and I clicked away throughout the day. I stopped off and picked up some souvenirs for Mona and Charmaine, while Lionel picked up a little something for his parents.

We spent the rest of the weekend relaxing and taking in as many sights as possible around Orlando. We decided to spend Sunday evening having a quiet little dinner in one of the resort's restaurants. Lionel must have coughed up some serious dough because the place was almost empty. I was having a nervous feeling about this, but wasn't sure why.

We had fried calamari for an appetizer. Lionel had the marinated pork chops and I had a petite filet. Nothing like a hunk of beef to get my strength back up after all the weekend's "activities".

Lionel was drinking iced tea and took a sip before asking, "Had a good time, Glover?"

"Good time? A great time, honey. I'm in heaven here. This is incredible, Lionel."

"Good. I'm glad you're in heaven and you know what? I don't want you to come down . . . ever, baby."

I noticed our waiter standing in the distance watching our table curiously. I was focused on the waiter, so I didn't notice the small box Lionel pulled from out of nowhere. When I looked back, all I heard was . . .

"Glover, will you marry me?" My world froze. I knew this was coming, but I had tried to put it out of my head. Were my doubts or fears that strong? If so, what was I doing stringing this good black man along?

"Glover? Did you hear me?"

"I'm, I'm sorry. Yes. Yes! I'll marry you!" And with that I welled up and the tears erupted. As I bawled like a baby, my thoughts were of my dear mother instead of this moment. The waiter had come forward from his vantage point and had brought out champagne as the rest of the staff stood around us and applauded. We would be returning to Los Angeles the next day, officially engaged and ready to take the next step. Lord, what was I doing?

16   *Max*

I was tempted to call Diane over the weekend, but I decided it was best to put that whole production behind me. Gawd, I needed to find the right woman for me. I never gave Smitty the whole story about Friday night. I felt terrible about almost going along with Jay and didn't want Smit to know what an ass he was. Jay was blood and had done right by me since my moving here, so I knew we would be talking eventually. Just not now.

Monday night at Denny's came and went with no Jay and no problems. I broke out of my sleep early Tuesday morning. I was dead tired, but I was off this day. Time for the job search again, but this time we were going downtown. I pulled my best interview suit from the closet. The suit was still wrapped in the plastic from the dry cleaners. I pulled my black Florsheims out of the back of the closet and dusted them off. I pulled out my resumes and organized them on my coffee table along with the various cover letters. I heard the State of California was hiring as well, so I had to make my way over to the Employment Development Office also. I stepped out my door with briefcase in hand and ready to take on the world. The navy blue with gray pinstripes was hitting with my burgundy silk tie and white Perry Ellis showing from underneath. I called Smitty before heading out and he met me by my Celica. Smitty had his papers in a folder and was standing there with his white button-down, salt and pepper slacks, and a gray and black tie.

"Check you out, *Maxwell!* You look like you plan on takin' you a job!"

"One can hope, my brother!"

We got underway a little late, so traffic was a little less hectic as we came in on I-10 heading east. Our plan was to crash in on the CBD and to try to get into as many places as possible. More planning would have been a good idea, but I was getting a little desperate. I had a map of downtown and circled which buildings I was going to visit. My goal was to land an entry-level position at one of the businesses and to work my way up into management. I wasn't too picky as to what type of business though. Smitty had his own places in mind, so we planned on working straight through lunch then meeting back at the car that afternoon.

I decided to try out the Gas Company Tower first. There were businesses like Nalcon, Intrix, and Barnes & Greenwood located there, which I had heard of back in Lake Charles. I was trying not to be impressed by all the success around me, but I couldn't hold back the grin that was plastered on my face. All I needed was a chance. I went over to the building index and formed a plan to cover as many businesses as possible in the place. I was sure that I would face a lot of rejection before the day was over, but it wouldn't stop me. All I needed was one success of my own. I chose to start with Nalcon on the forty-eighth floor. Might as well start at the top, or near it.

I was doing some people watching in the plaza as I waited for the elevator to descend to the lobby. A middle aged Asian woman in a black business suit smiled at me as she walked past. I wondered if she could tell that I was an outsider in their midst. The elevator opened and I boarded it along with five others. There was an Hispanic courier with a radio on his hip, a middle-aged Hispanic gentleman in a gray business suit, a thin white lady in a red business suit, this younger tanned white girl all in blue, and a bald brother in a olive colored suit. It was good to see a brother making it here and judging by his suit, he was doing pretty well for himself. I had first noticed the brother when we were down in the lobby. Mr. Clean had been holding a conversation with the girl in blue near me. I wasn't eavesdropping, but I could tell he was trying to calm her down about something. I guess they made up in the elevator, because they got in a quick kiss before getting off together on the thirtieth floor.

I actually managed to submit my resume and cover letter at Nalcon and completed an application. Some of the businesses in the building, like Barnes & Greenwood, weren't hiring or least told me that. All I could do was hope the phone call would come. I was drained by the time the afternoon rolled around, but Smitty still looked energized when he met me by the car.

"I got an interview next week, Max!" Smitty had loosened his tie and looked like he was ready to celebrate. I was ready to crawl back under my covers.

"Congrats, my brother! With who? When?"

"West-tel, dawg. It's only a mail and filing position, but it pays lot more than what I make now and I can move up. I have to come back for the interview, but it seems almost like a sure thing, y'know! I might be able to get a decent ride finally. How'd things go with you?"

"Nothing certain, Smit. But enough about me, let's get out of here and celebrate!"

I yanked my tie off and threw it in the back of the car along with my briefcase and jacket. We were heading down Sixth Street and were laughing it up when I remembered that I hadn't picked up a state employment application.

"I guess I can pick that up another day."

"Man, you better pick up that app now. Remember, the deadline is this Friday. Besides, that may be your lucky break."

"Yeah. I had forgotten about the deadline."

I turned the Celica around and headed for First Street. I spotted the LA Times building first on the right, then noticed the employment office in its shadow. Smitty decided to recline in the car, while I ran in to pick up the app.

The office was almost empty when I walked in and there were no workers in sight, which reminded me of the office at home. If the applications were handy, I would have simply picked one up and headed out the door. They weren't though. I decided to wait at the counter for a couple of minutes. I was about to head out the door in frustration when I caught a glimpse of someone zipping by in the back.

"Excuse me!" I hollered in the general direction of the blur I saw. The blur slowed, then hesitated. What a blur it was. Out walks this gorgeous sister. About 5'6, light brown with the eyes to match, and wearing this gold colored jacket and skirt that really showed just how fine she was. Her brown hair had some highlights in it and this piece was dangling over one eye. I don't know if the dangling was intentional though, but it pointed down almost perfectly to this little beauty mark on her cheek. Yep, I was taking it all in.

The blur opened her lovely mouth and said, "Can I help you?"

"Umm. Hi. I need an application." I had blanked out for a second and forgot what I was there for.

"For . . . ?" The look on her face told me she didn't have time for this. I was on the receiving end of a little bit of attitude.

"For the state jobs. I was told the applications could be picked up at any of the Employment Development Offices." I was phrasing my statement almost like a question in hopes that it would make a light bulb go off in the blur's head.

"Oh, okay. I don't normally work up here. The girl called in sick today and another one quit. I'll try to find it for you." The blur's tone had softened. She probably had her mind on other things. The sister started looking behind the counter and came up with the application in hand.

"Thank you."

"You're welcome. Don't forget . . . it needs to be in by this Friday." Aww. The blur could be courteous and helpful when given a chance.

"Oh, don't worry. I won't forget. I need the work," I said with a chuckle.

"Well, I hope you find the work you're looking for," the blur playfully replied. Her remark seemed almost flirtatious, but the rock on her hand told me otherwise. Oh well.

Strange though, I would have thought that someone with ice like that on her hand would be waving it around more. I had actually caught a lucky glimpse when she came up with the application and it almost blinded me .

"Later," I replied as I excused myself. To make myself feel good; I imagined her eyes on me as I headed out the door. Yeah. Right. Cheap thrills mean nothing. I looked back to confirm that I was being a little kid. Yep. There was the empty counter again. The blur had moved on and I was still an idiot.

17 *Glover*

I returned from Orlando officially engaged. *Really* engaged. And I had the ring to prove it. Lionel liked to be in control and had more than the proposal planned out as I found out later that evening. We had gone dancing after dinner that night and returned to the room, where we made love. I never faked an orgasm my entire time with Lionel . . . until that night. As Lionel held me in his arms, I cried. They weren't tears of joy as Lionel probably thought they were. Lionel then informed me of his (and his mom's) wedding plans. Catalina Island, the first place Lionel took me. Lionel had already talked it over with his mother, Adele, and she would be able to arrange everything for us once we selected a date. Hell, she would probably rent the whole fucking island. Adele probably would have preferred a church wedding, but Lionel knew how I felt about churches. I was numb still as I stared down at the diamond on my finger and when I blurted out "no time like the present".

We were to be married on Catalina Island in three months.

The cab stopped at my apartment Monday night and Lionel carried my luggage and walked me in. It was late and we both had to get back into the swing of things on Tuesday. I had no idea how much of a roller coaster Tuesday would be.

I came in Tuesday morning to find out that one of the girls at work had walked off the job the day before and another was out sick. My desk had stacks of files on it and I was to be married in three months. This Tuesday had a "Monday" feel to it.

Mona and Charmaine rushed to my desk before I even had a chance to put my purse down.

Mona squinted at me and said, "Bitch, you came in last night and didn't even call me to tell me? Let me see that ring!"

I held it up for them to see. Charmaine was silent for a full four seconds. A new record.

"Oh my gawd!!!!!!! The size of that diamond! Do you know how much this must have cost?"

"I think I do," Mona chimed in. She probably did have an idea of how much it cost.

"C'mon y'all. It's just an engagement ring," I said trying to convince myself. This was a big piece of ice on my hand. I was starting to get self-conscious.

"Okay! Okay! Enough about the ring! How many times did you do the nasty? Do you have a date set? We want the dirt," Charmaine cackled with delight. Mona was actually in agreement with her this time.

"I'm not answering your first question, you nasty wench! As for your other question, well . . . the wedding's going to be in Catalina . . . in three months."

Both Mona and Charmaine were caught off guard with that announcement. Mona and I exchanged looks that spoke of our conversation at her condo that Friday night.

"Oh, and don't worry! I brought y'all some souvenirs back, but I forgot them at the apartment this morning."

The rest of the day was less than peachy. Mr. Marx, the office supervisor, was on the warpath with us being understaffed. In addition to playing catch-up on my own desk, I was expected to fill in wherever needed. That, combined with the jet lag did not make for a happy Glover. Yep. A lot of shit on my mind.

Lionel called me from his office to see if I was up for lunch, but I took a raincheck. I was trying to clear my desk and my head as well. Lionel had to be stupid not to realize that I was acting differently since "the question". I had decided on working through lunch. Charmaine and Mona trekked off on their own to get some shopping in after they gave up on me.

Lunch came and went in a blur. I was deep into my work and lost in deep thought at the same time. Did I love Lionel? If I didn't, then why was I marrying him? We had been dating for over two years, so was this the next logical step? I guess I had issues.

I heard, "Excuse me!" as I walked near the front of the office. Somebody had walked in from off the street. Damn. I didn't work in the front and really didn't feel like going up there. I slowed down and considered continuing toward the other end of the office. That wasn't my style though. I broke off from the direction I was heading and approached the front counter.

The voice belonged to one heck of a good-looking brother. He was wearing a white shirt with navy blue suit pants and looked like he had a rough day at the office. He was brown skinned and not as tall as Lionel, but with some little bulges beneath his shirt. I could tell his eyes were scanning me as I approached, but he had something different in his smile and tired eyes. He seemed a little less "wolflike" than most brothers, if there is such a thing.

"Can I help you?"

"Umm. Hi. I need an application." He seemed a little slow and I had work to do.

"For . . .?"

He told me he was looking for the state employment applications. I apologized for not knowing where things were and explained about our being short staffed and stuff. I really didn't know why I was volunteering all that info. I found the application and handed it to him, being sure to remind him of the Friday deadline.

"Oh, don't worry. I won't forget. I need the work," he replied with that smile. He laughed, but it didn't hide the exhaustion behind it.

"Well, I hope you find the work you're looking for," just spilled out of my mouth. Why did I say that?!! My intention was to just be courteous, but it came out playful, almost kittenish. His facial expression didn't change so I was relieved. I guess I hadn't embarrassed myself, . . . unless that was his poker face. He took the application and began walking off. My eyes went to lock in on his ass, but his shirt had come out of his pants in the back. My view of the buns was blocked. I lingered at the counter for a second more for reasons unknown to me. I had a devilish grin on my face, then looked down at the ring on my hand. Time for reality to kick in again. He did have a nice smile though and had given me a brief escape from my issues. But it was time to finish the job I was doing before "smiley" interrupted me. Hmm. I never got his name. I moved on to the back, but took one last peek before he made it all the way out the door.

18 *Max*

An entire day had passed and the blur was on my mind. Still. This time, she was washing my Celica in a pair of ass cutters . . . and everything was in black and white. Suds and shit everywhere. Maybe I shouldn't have watched that Maria video before going to bed last night. I considered telling Smitty about her, but felt pretty stupid about the whole thing. Smitty either would have laughed his ass off or would have gone inside the place to get a look see. I had too many distractions occurring lately. I did need to finish the application before tomorrow and there was no time like the present. I walked over to my stereo and put on my old Zagora CD. Nothing like "Stay a Little While, Child" to take me away from all the crap. I found a pen under the table and plopped down on the couch. Might as well start at the beginning with "name".

My phone rang, catching me off guard.

I reached over and hit the talk button. "Hello?"

"Hi. Max?" It was a female voice that I couldn't place. I flew off the couch to turn the stereo down.

"Yeah! It's me . . . "

"It's Valerie. How are ya?" I could hear the smile in her voice although it was a nervous one.

"Fine! I'm fine! And you?" I had plopped back down and was resting the phone on my shoulder. I was determined to bring the app back today.

"I'm okay, Max. You know, I've been thinking about you. I was wondering if you were going to call. Probably not, huh?"

"Oh, I was planning on calling you. I've just been busy with work and all." I don't *think* I just told a lie.

"I see. Are you working tonight? I thought maybe we could *see* each other . . . " I had reached the line on the application to check off "married" or "single". I started thinking about the ring on the blur's finger. I wonder what her name was.

"Max? Are you listening?"

"Yeah . . . I'm sorry. I'm trying to fill out something, that's all."

"Sooooooo?" I must have missed something she said. Uh oh.

"So?"

"So, can we see each other tonight?" Damn. I had missed that completely.

"Ooo. Tonight's bad, Valerie," I responded. "I'm about to head out the door and I'm not sure what time I'll be back. Raincheck?"

"Raincheck." I was the *last* person who needed to be giving out nookie rainchecks.

"Alright. I'll call you. Maybe we can do something this weekend?"

"Yeah. That'd be nice. Take care, Max."

"You too."

I grabbed my sunglasses and headed out the door with the application. I then ran back in and grabbed a resume. The Santa Monica Freeway was calling out to me.

I made my way downtown without getting pulled over by five-oh. The employment office was busier this time. I guess everybody was coming in at the last minute.

No blur in sight when I walked in. Another sister was at the front counter. Good looking as well. Did they grow them in here? I waited nervously in line. I was feeling like I was back in high school and waiting for my prom date to walk out. I moved up to the counter.

"May I help you?" Damn. Her words rolled out so crisply. They put a very polished sister up here.

"Yeah. I'm dropping off the application for the state job openings. I wanted to make it in before tomorrow." I was looking toward the back area as I spoke. Maybe I would catch a glance.

"Okay. Do you have a resume also?"

"Right underneath," I pointed out while still looking away.

"Alright. Did you need anything else?" The sister was looking at me suspiciously. I hope she didn't think I was a terrorist or anything.

"No. That's it. Thank you."

19 *Glover*

My alarm went off Friday morning, as usual. I was always interrupted from getting my groove on with Taye. Nothing new, except this time it wasn't Taye. In my dream, I couldn't make out the face. It was all a blur. I had to be at work in an hour and didn't have time to mess around with dreams. I threw my T-shirt in the dirty clothes hamper, put my shower cap on and dove into the shower.

I stood there under the spray with my eyes closed. Water rolled down my body and steam hovered in the air around me while in a dazed state. A sharp breeze of cold air hit me, causing goosebumps to pop up all over. I then felt them. The pair of hands came up slowly from behind me and grasped me by my hips. I knew I had to be to work, but this was feeling pretty good. I didn't open my eyes because I was afraid it would end. The hands slowly worked themselves across my stomach then headed upwards in tiny circular motions. The hands were caressing my breasts and I started biting my bottom lip. The water was splashing me all over and I was starting to splash inside. The hands then plunged down between my legs causing me to fall backwards and into a hard body. As I felt fingers entering me, all I could think of was a face. And a smile.

From behind me, a deep voice whispered, "Forgot me in the bed, huh?"

I spun around in shock to see Lionel's face in front of me. As we stood there under the spray, I realized that he was right. I had forgotten him in the bed. I had let him stay the night and had completely forgotten. I was really in the shower and this was real.

I made it to work a little bit late. I insisted that I drive myself to work. Mr. Marx had put Mona working the front until our personnel problems were solved. Charmaine was still bitching when I came in.

"G-love, I'm gonna plant my foot in that white mutherfucker's ass."

"Charmaine . . . you're white."

"Oh hush! You know what I mean! Mr. Marx told Mona that she was gonna be up front for another week."

"Alright, Charmaine. I need to get started on my desk. The DMV has a few openings and I have to get to work on these files."

"You do that, girl. I'm not bustin' my ass for anyone today. It's Friday and I just got paid. You really should get direct deposit too." With that said, Charmaine marched off to file things with a smile.

I sat down at my desk and started looking over files of potential hires to pass on to the DMV. Then a wild thought hit me. I got up from my desk and walked up to the front. Mona must have taken a break. I walked over to the application bins behind the counter. I looked around with a guilty look on my face then stooped down behind the counter. I started rifling through the most recent state employment applications. They were date stamped so it was easy to go through those that had been just returned. For all I knew, the particular one I was looking for may not have been there. I didn't even have a name to go on. I was interrupted or caught when I heard a voice behind me.

"Looking for something, Ms. McDaniel?" Mona was standing there looking at me with an accusing eye even though she hadn't a clue. She liked making people uncomfortable and I was easy pickings right now. I was probably blushing.

"Oh, nothing really," I replied as I managed to keep a straight face with my hand in the cookie jar, "Just taking a look at the apps for those state jobs."

"Oh. Today's the last day. I hope they're finished bringing them in. I have to send them off to Sacramento later on. People really started pouring in yesterday with the apps, even this cute brother."

"*Oh?*" My eyebrow raised. "I'm surprised you didn't try to make him your newest slave. What was wrong with him? Too short? Gold tooth?"

"No. There was nothing really wrong with him physically. Around six foot, nice little bod, and stuff. Nice smile. Just the nervous sort . . . kept looking around. Like he was casing the place or something."

"Oh. I see. Nice smile, huh?" Bingo.

20

Max

I don't know what I was doing at Del Amo Mall that Friday. I had stopped in at Denny's to check the work schedule. I was working the weekend. Samir took care of the brother, but he had to put me on the weekend schedule sometimes. Besides, I probably would have wound up in some kind of trouble. Nothing like good, hard work to clear a man's head. I drove across the street and found Jay's Bimmer in its usual spot on the mall parking lot. He must have opened the store this morning.

We hadn't spoken since the night at Captains. My weak ass was starting to feel bad. I didn't agree with what Jay did, but I didn't want to let everything end on that note. He was blood. My mom had taught me the importance of your peoples. I bopped on into the mall entrance by the food court and went up the escalator. Male Tree was on the left at the top.

There were a few customers looking around, but no Jay in sight. He must have been in the back or on break. I decided to hang out for a second and browsed through some of the shirts on the "sale" rack. I was looking for an extra-large when I heard Jay's voice. He was at the register ringing up a customer. He must have gone in the back to get something for the dude at the register. He had to have seen me when he came back out, but he was wearing his work face. Jay was still trying to get that extra sale, whether it be a pair of socks, a tie, or whatever. I waited for him to finish the sale before approaching the counter.

65

"Whaddup, cuz."

"Whaddup with you, Country?" His intention was to bother me, but it wasn't working this time.

"Nothing. I was on this end checking my schedule and saw your ride. You stayin' outta trouble?" That was a stupid question on my part, but it helped to break the tension between us.

Jay smirked and shot back, "You ever gonna *get* in any trouble, Country? Man, I'm ashamed to call you my cousin sometimes. That was some foul shit, nigga."

"Foul?! How in the hell was I foul? You were the one up there lying and shit. Then you . . . " I had to pause as I was starting to talk loud and there were still customers in the store. "Then you tried to ditch Smitty and shit. You know that was wrong, man."

"Alright. Alright. You got me there. I had no choice though. Those bitches were callin' and I was ready to pick up the phone. Cuz, you should have been there," said Jay with a big grin that told everything. Jay then started stroking his goatee with pride. I stopped my imagination, as I didn't need to be thinking about the three of them together . . . and my ass standing alone outside Captains.

"Whatever, Jay. Hey look, I'm gonna run. I gotta go home and get some rest before tonight. You take care of yourself."

"Always, cousin! Always," said Jay with a laugh as he strolled over to assist a customer. A female customer. Jay would always be Jay.

I put the windows down and turned up Power 106 on the way home. Mr. Choc was cutting up with the hip-hop party mix this afternoon. I probably looked silly with all the head nodding I did on the 405. It didn't matter because I loved music and the escape it gave me. I passed up the apartment when I realized that I was riding on "E" and filled up the Celica at the Union Seventy-Six further up Venice Boulevard. While I was there paying for the gas, I picked up a turkey sandwich. I'd get something else at work that evening. I finished the sandwich off on the way back to my apartment.

After I got back in, I headed straight for the bedroom to catch some Z's. I threw my clothes on the chair and clicked on the thirteen inch on my dresser. I sprawled across the bed while watching Judge Judy scream at another weak fool. I let out a laugh as I began to drift off. I clicked the TV off just as I prepared to go unconscious and turned on my side. I caught the flicker of light from my answering machine right as my eyes closed and suddenly reopened them. I started to let the message keep until after my nap, but decided against it. It might be something important.

I pushed the "message" button and waited for the tape to play. It was a woman's voice.

"*Ummm. This is the California Employment Development Office downtown. I am calling for Mr. Maxwell Guillory. You completed an application recently for one of the state openings. I know you may not be interested in this based on your qualifications, but the DMV has some openings to fill as well. Please call if you would be available to come by our office on First Street this Monday around eleven o'clock a.m. for a pre-screening interview.*"

21 Glover

I was pulling some stupid, crazy shit and had spent all weekend trying to talk myself out of it. It didn't work. Friday, I went through the applications that were dropped off the day before. I found three applications that could have matched what I was looking for. Mona had no idea that she had helped me out with this.

Monday was the day. I showed up to work wearing my royal blue three-piece skirt set. Of the three applications I had pulled, two of them agreed to come in for the DMV "pre-screening interview". I hadn't heard from the third. The interview was a half-truth anyway. With my job, I had the authority to do some interviewing for the DMV openings, but never actually had. I would usually just review the files of registered job seekers and forward those that might be compatible with the employer's needs. The applications that I had pulled and reviewed were for people seeking higher paying state jobs. I didn't want to block that, so I just made copies of the two applications. Even though my intentions were less than noble, I did plan on forwarding my pre-screening results to the DMV.

My first interview was set up for ten o'clock a.m. I had cleared my desk and had told Mona that I was expecting some interviewees. Mona had replied with a "Huh?" and then followed up with a "Whatever." She was still less than enthusiastic about working the front, but did come get me when the ten o'clock showed up. The first interviewee was a twenty-four year old brother. He was wearing those micro-dreads in his head and was polite as hell. He wasn't the person I was looking for, but I thought he would be a great hire based on his interview. While I was interviewing him, I could see Charmaine making faces at me behind his back. Charmaine couldn't wait to run up when the first interview was finished.

"Girl, what in the *hell* are you doing?"

I playfully replied, "I don't know what you're talking about, Charmaine."

"First your ass shows up here dressed all professional and then you're holding interviews? Girl, you up to somethin'. You *are* gonna fill me in, huh?"

"I'm not sure myself and you probably would be better off not knowing. Can't I just be doing my job?"

Charmaine shot back, "Bitch, *please.*"

Mona walked up and interjected, "Ms. McDaniel, your *next* interview is here." Mona then cast an accusing stare on me. Her eyes told me that she had a better understanding of what had gone down last Friday. She still was in the dark, but she could see the light under the door. Mona was feeling played, but wasn't sure how.

I walked out to meet the last interviewee, greeted him, and then escorted him back to my desk past a suspicious Mona. After I offered him a seat at my desk, we began to get into the interview.

"Well, I'm glad you received my message last Friday. I've reviewed your state application, but why don't you tell me some more about yourself . . . Mr. Nelson."

Number two was another good candidate and I would forward his information on as well.

Maybe that was some consolation for making a fool of myself and trying to scheme. Here I was engaged to be married and trying to create a "situation" to meet the brother with the nice smile from last Tuesday. Serves me right for none of the two interviewees being him. I wasn't even positive that he had returned the application. For someone normally confident and in control, I had been doing some stupid shit lately. Charmaine and Mona had gone on to lunch without me as I was still interviewing number two. My strange behavior was probably their hot topic over lunch.

I was feeling foolish and dejected as I threw my purse on my shoulder. I decided to have lunch across the street at the little diner. I needed the walk to clear my head. I punched out and dragged my feet as I headed for the front door. I was looking down at a scuff mark on one of my pumps and didn't see the door swinging open.

Bang! The door bumped me in the head slightly as I caught a glimpse of a gray pant leg and black loafers.

"Oh! I'm sorry! Are you okay?"

"I'm fine. I'm . . . " It was him. The smile was there and the eyes didn't seem tired this time. He was wearing a gray suit and looking all GQ'd this time.

"I got a call Friday for an interview and I know I'm running late. Do you know who I'm supposed to see?"

"Umm, that would be me. I'm the one who called. You must be *number thr* . . . I mean. You must be Mr. Guillory?" His was the application that I hadn't heard from.

"Right! Call me Max," he said with a burst of enthusiasm.

"Well, I'm heading to lunch right now. Care to join me, Max?"

"It's the least I could do, since I hit you with the door, Ms . . ."

"Glover. Call me Glover."

22

Max

I tried to call the employment office after I got over the shock of my message. I was too late. The office was closed. The DMV wasn't what I had in mind, but I couldn't be too choosy. I was working the weekend, so I had to call the employment office first thing Monday morning. When I got to Denny's that night, I realized that I hadn't looked at Monday's schedule. I was scheduled for work that morning. Samir agreed to let me off a little early, so I could make it downtown in time. Now I was sitting at lunch in a diner with the blur. Turned out her name was Glover and she was looking as beautiful as ever. Too bad she was taken. I had a double burger and fries, while she had soup and salad.

"Again, I'm sorry about the door back there. I knew I was late, so I was rushing. I'm still new to the area, so I'm afraid to try shortcuts when traffic backs up."

"Oh? You not from here, huh? New to L.A. or new to California all together?"

"New to California. I moved here from Louisiana about six months ago. Do you have any relatives from there?" I decided to quiz her a little.

"No. Most of my relatives are from Virginia. Around Arlington and Fredericksburg. My mother used to take me out there to visit . . . before she passed away. Why'd you ask about Louisiana?"

"No reason really. You look like you could be from out there. The funny eyes made me think about that! What are they exactly? Light brown? Hazel?"

"Whatever you want to call them, Max," she replied with that lovely mouth of hers. She then reached over and helped herself to one of my fries. The sight of that ring on her hand snapped me back to reality again. We hadn't discussed any business yet.

"Um. I called this morning to let you know I was coming in, but the girl who answered didn't know what I was talking about."

"That doesn't surprise me. I should have left my direct number on your answering machine. You're looking good today," she said while looking over my suit.

"Oh! You mean compared to the other day when you saw me," I blurted out. "I was a little rough then. I had been all over downtown that day and was dead tired."

"No, you were fine that day. Tell me, would you really be interested in one of the openings at the DMV?"

"To tell you the truth, I'm probably looking for more than what they're offering, but you have to start somewhere. What made you call me for the opening?"

"What made you come down here for the interview," she shot back. Glover seemed a little nervous for a second. It was like she was avoiding my question.

"Oh! Ms. Glover doesn't want to answer my question, huh?" I was starting to feel comfortable around this woman.

"No! It's not that! It . . . it's just that I'm the one that is supposed to be asking the questions here. That's all!" Her playfulness was coming out. I was *really* feeling this woman.

I said, "Okay. I apologize. Can I ask one more question, . . . *ma'am*?"

"Yes you may, *sir*," she responded.

"How did you get your name? A girl named Glover. It's different."

"Yeah, it is different. I was named after my great-grandmother. And by the way . . . that's a *woman* named

Glover," she corrected me. I nodded my understanding as I got lost in her eyes.

"So Mr. Guillory, is there a special someone in your life out here . . . or in Louisiana?"

"Umm. No. Just going through the motions right now. We all can't be as lucky as you," I said while glancing down at the rock on Glover's hand.

"Oh. Okay," she said with a smile. I had bothered her with that remark, but didn't know why. Was the ring just a front to keep the brothers at bay? Was I having lunch with a player? More importantly, was I playing myself?

"This is a really good burger! Oh . . . and by the way . . . you owe me for that French fry you took earlier."

Glover replied, "Well, maybe I'll have the chance to return the favor in the future." Our eyes met right then and I knew I was playing a dangerous game.

"Just make sure the fries are hot. I hate cold fries."

"Yessir! Hot fries, sir! Coming, sir! Haha!"

"Are you usually this silly, Glover?"

"No. But I have you to thank for that. Thanks."

"For what?"

"Just for being here. I know the only reason we are sitting here is because of the interview, but you've really helped me forget about some things that are going on right now. So I just wanted to say 'Thank You.'" I was watching her lips in slow motion just then.

"Things are going that bad right now?" I inquired.

"No. Things are just complicated. That's all." I knew not to push the subject. If she wanted to open up she would do it on her own. I sat back in my seat.

"So, what do I do now? About the opening, that is. Do you need me to go back to the office and sign anything?"

"No. I'll forward your info to the DMV and it'll be up to them. Your application for the state jobs was sent off to Sacramento with the rest last week. And that's it," she said with a sigh. It seemed like she didn't want the lunch to end. Our plates had already been cleared and I was putting the money on the table.

"Okay. Well let me walk you back to your office then." As Glover walked ahead of me, my eyes were watching the curve of her hips through the tight blue skirt she was wearing.

We made the walk back across the street and stopped in front of her office. Her look told me not to follow her in and that this was the place to say goodbye. We stood there smiling with no words said before she let out a "Thank you." again. I wanted to take this stranger in my arms and feel those lips against mine, but gave her a polite handshake instead.

"Sorry about your mother."

"Huh?"

"You mentioned your mother passing away."

"Y . . . yes. I did, didn't I? Well, thank you. Again." She had a confused look on her face, but the smile was genuine. Glover then disappeared through the door and was gone like a blur . . . again.

23

Glover

I did all I could to keep myself busy during the rest of the week. Anything to keep Max off my mind. I was spending Saturday with Lionel, so me and the girls decided to have a sleepover Friday night. I decided to hold it at my apartment this time, since the last few were at Mona's and Charmaine's.

Charmaine brought the coolers, Mona brought the movies and music, and I cooked the dinner. I brought some of my secret fried chicken to work one day and the gang had been bothering me ever since. I promised to take care of my girls. I bought the fresh chicken and left it marinating Thursday night, just like my mom had taught me. I learned the recipe while standing at my mom's side as a little girl and had committed it to memory. People loved my chicken although I never thought it could touch mom's. I cheated with the store-bought potato salad from the store, but I did toss a fresh green salad.

Mona showed up in jeans and a T-shirt with her shades up on her head. Her overnight bag was dangling over her shoulder. She went straight to work on the entertainment and put on some Eric Benet, while setting up the VCR for later. Charmaine came banging on the door less than five minutes later in her jogging suit. After putting the coolers in the fridge, Charmaine helped set the table. We got our grub on right after the chicken was pulled out of the grease and barely gave it time to cool.

The three of us waddled toward the TV on full stomachs after leaving the table. Charmaine stopped for a second to let out a little belch that was followed by a little giggle and an "excuse me". Charmaine staked out the couch as her territory. Mona and I sprawled out across my Persian rug that I had picked up from the swap meet.

"Mona, what movies did you rent?"

"Why?" Mona answered with one of her fake innocent faces.

"Aw shit. She done gone and rented 'Mahogany' again," Charmaine screamed out.

"*Mona* . . . tell me you didn't rent that again."

"What's wrong with Mahogany, y'all?"

Charmaine answered, "Nothing . . . if you like watching that shit again . . . "

"And again!" I chimed in. "Why can't you rent 'The Bodyguard' sometimes instead, Mona? Since you're so big on divas and stuff. "

"That's a good movie too, but I want to see the original *diva*. No fakes allowed."

"Okay, Mona. We gotta watch something else tonight. It's fun to watch Billy Dee's radical, protestin' ass, but not tonight. Okay?"

Mona rolled her eyes then gave up. I took that time to grab some coolers from the kitchen. "Y'all ready for some drinks?" They didn't answer. I could hear them whispering by the couch. I decided to bring them a cooler as well. When I walked out, Mona and Charmaine were grinning.

Charmaine started off, "Glover, we've been wondering. Do you plan on asking us to be in your wedding? It'll be here before you know it and you haven't really brought it up. We've noticed that you've been kinda *distracted* at work with interviews and all." The two of them started snickering.

"What the fuck is so funny?"

"Nothing, Ms. McDaniel. You've just seemed *different* since you came back from Orlando. Like your mind is somewhere else," Mona replied.

"I'm gonna be married in less than three months and you're wondering why I'm acting different? Damn! Wouldn't you be?!" I was getting defensive. My voice was rising.

"Calm down, G-love! We just noticed the way you were acting the other day, when you were interviewing those dudes. That, and how you never talk about the wedding and stuff. It seems almost like you don't want to be married."

"Hey! Why are y'all all up in my business like that? What am I supposed to do? Run around singing and shit?"

Mona and Charmaine sat there with their eyes blinking and looking embarrassed. The room was silent as the CD player was switching to another disc. I knew exactly what Mona and Charmaine were getting at, but didn't want to deal with it now.

Mona chose to break the silence. "Glover, there's no need to blow up like that. We were just worried about you. We didn't mean to upset you, girl."

"I'm okay. I'm just under a lot of stress. It was stupid of me to forget . . . will you guys be in my wedding? Please?"

Charmaine answered, "Hell yeah! You think we would pass up the chance to walk down an aisle with some more good-looking brothers like Lionel? Shiiiiiit!" We all laughed.

I asked, "Charmaine, do you have something else in you? Besides white, I mean. Cause you sure do love you some black men. Your shape is even a little different. I've been dying to ask since we first met. What's up with that?"

"Well, if you must know. My dad's American Indian and my mom's Italian American. I took my mom's last name, Fulda. My dad was never really around much."

"I know all about that Charmaine. My father skipped out when I was little. I couldn't even tell you where he is now. And here I thought you were just a crazy white girl from the Valley!"

"Fuck you too, bitch! Now you know that I'm just a half-crazy white girl! Or would that be 'crazy half-white girl'? And watch that 'Valley' shit. You know I wasn't raised there."

"Okay! Okay! A half-crazy white girl from Crenshaw! Haha!"

Mona was feeling uncomfortable now. Our talk about fathers had bothered her. Her father was always in the scene. The problem was that Mona considered him an asshole. Especially after he left her mom.

I broke the tension with, "So are y'all gonna drink your coolers or what? It's the least you could do . . . since you're gonna be in my wedding. Now give me love!"

After the big group hug, we moved on to other things and even put on Mona's other rental. We started winding down in the early morning hours. Charmaine was snoring now under her blanket. Mona was in my bathroom putting on her night mask and pajamas. I sat up to gather the empty cooler bottles and to throw them away in the kitchen. I was standing there in the dark when I almost jumped out of my skin.

"We saw you the other day."

It was Mona. She was behind me in her silk pajamas. She was standing in the entranceway to the kitchen and had scared the hell out of me. The green shit on her face didn't help.

"Huh?"

"Me and Charmaine saw you Monday. In front of the office with your friend. Wasn't that the cutie I had told you about?" Damn.

"Yeah. He was one of the interviews. He got there late." It was pitch black, but I still was avoiding eye contact.

"Just be careful, Ms. McDaniel. Alright?" Mona then turned and walked off.

24

Max

"Open up, nigga!" Smitty was banging on my door Friday afternoon. I swear, one day he was going to get evicted with his loud ass. I had been hanging around the apartment in my boxers and didn't expect any company. I had barely opened the door when Smitty barged on in past me. He was wearing a suit so I knew what that meant.

"You got the job at West-tel, huh?"

"Yeah, nigga! You damn right! Mr. Wallace Lewis is now fully employed! They even take care of my parking and shit. That'll come in handy once I get a dependable ride. Damn. You still in your boxers?"

"They look good to me." At the sound of the voice, I spun around to see a heavy-set sister in my doorway. She had a lollipop in her mouth and was looking at me with a wicked smile. She was brown-skinned and was wearing a white blouse with a pair of blue denim shorts. Her gold earrings were dangling just below her brand new weave. It was Zena, one of Smitty's women. She must have given him a ride downtown. I scurried off toward my bedroom to put something on.

"Oh don't put anything on, on my account. I'm just enjoying the view. Heh. Heh," Zena said as she closed my apartment door behind her.

"Hi, Zena," I said as I ducked into my room with my embarrassed ass.

"Hey, baby! Heh. Heh." Zena was making herself comfortable on my couch and she checked out my apartment. She had never been inside.

"Ay! Ay, girl! You tryin' to make me jealous up in here?" I could see Smitty lean over from behind the couch and wrap his arms around Zena.

"Smit, you know I'm just havin' a little fun with Max. You know he can't do nothin' for me, boo." Zena then leaned back and gave Smitty a kiss. They liked to play the lovebird game when they were together, but both of them were doing their own thing most of the time. I think they both liked it that way.

Smitty hollered, "Hurry up, Max! Put some clothes on your ass and shit. We're gonna get our celebration eat on. "

I threw on a pair of my Girbauds with my white Nautica T-shirt and laced up my white Reebok soldiers. I could still hear Zena's giggling in the living room while I tightened the hair up in the mirror and put on my watch. I was in no rush to head back out there after the scene with my boxers. I would have taken longer, but this was my boy's time.

"Now what's this about getting our eat on?" I said as I walked back out.

"Me and Zena were thinking about heading over to Sizzler to celebrate, but then Zena changed her mind," said Smitty.

"Yeah. I want to go to Roscoe's, baby. We ain't been there in so long." Zena was licking her lips.

"I don't want to cramp you guys' style and shit. Why don't you two go on?"

"Nah, nigga. You my boy n' shit. Besides, I wouldn't have the job if it wasn't for you. You drove us down there that day, remember? C'mon! Zena's drivin'!"

We left my apartment and walked over to Zena's ride. Zena was pushing an arctic blue Mercury Mountaineer on some chrome eighteen inch rims. I was surprised she didn't have a personalized plate on it. We jumped in and were rolling up Venice Boulevard toward the Santa Monica Freeway. Zena had the windows down, the sunroof open, and her stereo blaring. All eyes on her. Smitty was sitting in the passenger seat up front and was leaning over the armrest toward Zena. I guess he was marking his turf to any busters that may be watching. Funny, Smitty still had his suit on. I guess he was enjoying the moment. I was in the back leaned back and was looking at the mini marts and stores we passed.

"Hey. We're going to the Roscoe's on Pico, right?"

"Max! Max! Starting to learn your way around, huh? Zena, you should have seen this nigga when he first got out here. He had his little maps and shit. Now this nigga knows his way around here better than me." Zena was smiling at Smitty as she threw her lollipop stick out the window and snatched a new one from the center console in one motion.

"Smit, have you told Home Stop yet?"

"Nah! I was thinking about not even telling them. Just up and leave em hanging, but that wouldn't be professional-like. I'm gonna put in my two weeks notice."

"Yep. My baby's a professional now," Zena chimed in as she looked over her shoulder to merge onto the freeway. "Hey, Max. Did Smitty tell you about my sister, Sonia? She broke up with her old man last week."

"Oh." Here it comes.

"Yeah. Anyway, she's lookin' for a new man. She's a little bit smaller than me, but just as cute. I know you ain't gay, so I was thinkin' about bringing Sonia with me next time I came over. You two would make a cute couple. I know you from down south and all, so you probably ain't used to sophisticated women like us. You probably used to them slower country girls back home, huh? Heh. Heh."

"Uh, yeah. It's been an adjustment." Smitty wasn't saying a thing. He had quietly slid back over to his side and was looking out his window. He knew this was coming up.

"Smitty, baby? Ain't y'all barbecuing at the apartment next week?" Shit. He told her about that.

Smitty acted startled and said, "Yeah, baby. We got a reason to 'cue' now." Mental note: kick Smitty's ass.

25 *Glover*

After learning that my best friends had discovered me making a fool of myself, I still slept pretty well. It must have been the coolers that helped. There wasn't a further mention from Mona about her revelation last night. I fixed a big breakfast for my girls before they headed out. Charmaine was headed back to the Valley and Mona was off for Santa Monica. That left me clear to go see my future husband, Lionel.

It was warmer than usual this morning, so I decided to use the air conditioning on the drive up to Lionel's. I guess global warming was to blame. I took one last look at myself in the mirror as I drove through Lionel's gate. Just to think, I would be living here in less than three months. As nice as it was, I was still uncomfortable. Kind of like a stranger.

I pulled my Civic in next to Lionel's Volvo. Lionel was at my car door before I got out and planted a big kiss on me. I chose to use that time to cop a feel on his ass.

"Nice to see it's still there. Hadn't grabbed it in a while."

"Where would it have gone? I missed you, Glover. I wish you were here last night, but I know you had plans with your girls and all. I need to be patient though. We're going to be with each other every night soon enough."

"Yep. Just don't be expecting me to have your meal cooked every night." I cut a smile at Lionel on that one.

Lionel gave me a gentle elbow and said, "And what's wrong with my woman cooking for me every night?"

"Nothing's wrong with it, Lionel. I'm just wondering what woman you're talking about."

"I see we're going to have to negotiate the terms of this marriage, huh?"

We walked into Lionel's place through the kitchen and came out into the front living room area. As I looked up at the vaulted ceiling, I wondered how long ago this house was built. I never was one for architecture. We wound up sitting at pool side in back. Lionel had a table out there and there was a nice breeze blowing from out of the North. A small tree was providing perfect shade for us. Lionel had gone back inside and came out with a couple of Snapples. He knew that fruit punch was my favorite. Stocking up for the Mrs. already.

"Glover, my mother wants to know if you're available Wednesday. She's trying to get the plans together."

"Yep. I can make it right after work." Lionel's expression changed for a second. He had something on his mind.

"You know you can leave your job at that place. I've told you that before. Tell me, do you plan on working there after we're married?"

"Lionel . . . I'm not sure, baby," I said as I sipped my Snapple. "We'll see."

"I'm not going to push that. Lord knows it wouldn't help. You're just so damn independent, but that's one of the things I love about you."

"Are you coming with me by your mother's?"

"Oh no! I know better. I plan on just showing up at the wedding looking good. I'll leave all the details to you women."

"You mean 'to your mother' don't you?"

"C'mon. I already talked to her about this. This is *our* wedding and she knows it. You need to give her a chance, baby."

"You're right. She *is* going to be my mother-in-law."

"So, have you thought about moving in yet? I've got all this space and it's sooooo lonely over here."

"Buy a fish, baby. You know I want to wait until we're married."

"Well, we're *almost* there."

"Hey! Once I'm living here, you'll probably be wishing for your single days! You know I've been eyeing your walk-in closet!"

"Once we're married, I'll give you a view of it from a different angle."

"Oh? Mr. Dunning, are you being a nasty boy?"

"Me?" he replied with those pretty teeth of his showing.

"Yeah! You!" Maybe this marriage thing wouldn't be that bad. Lionel and I got along great, but I honestly didn't know if he was the one that I loved. I still wasn't sure if it was real for me.

One thing I was very proud of though. I had gone an entire day without thinking about Mr. Maxwell Guillory. Oops.

26 *Max*

Zena left her Mountaineer with Smitty the next day. It was probably his reward for assisting her in trying to hook me up with Sonia. Smitty had some health club guest passes that were about to expire and we both had the day off. We were there. I needed to relieve some stress and hitting the weights was the right idea. Smitty just wanted to push Zena's ride in front of some honeys. I could tell Smitty was allergic to working out just by looking at his scrawny ass. He wouldn't admit it though.

"Damn, nigga. You're gonna put more weight on there?"

"Yeah. Just a little bit more. You not getting tired, huh Smit?"

"Me? Sheeet! I just don't want you hurtin' yourself."

"Oh. That's it, huh? Hey, what's up with that Sonia shit?"

"Aww, dawg. That was Zena's idea. Sonia saw you one day when her and Zena were going by my crib. I'm not in this shit, bro. Honest. Now, if you and Sonia happen to hook up . . . then . . . that's your business, bro. That crazy nigga she was foolin' with got put in the County."

"Oh! And you want *me* messin' with his woman? I may be new out here, but I'm not stupid."

"Nah, man. He's gonna be gone for a loooooong while. I heard she was a freak," Smitty said with a silly smile on his face.

"What? You did her, Smit?"

"Me? Hell no! Zena would kick my ass. No. She'd bust a cap in my ass."

"We're not gonna be hangin' like this anymore soon, man."

"Yeah. I'm gonna be working bankers hours in a couple of weeks. Hell, nigga . . . you gonna be working those hours soon enough too. Any word yet?"

"Smit, remember that day downtown. When I went in the employment office?"

"Yeah."

"I met this girl there. Beautiful."

"What? She was looking for a job in there too?"

"No, fool! She works there."

"Oh! That's what took your ass so long! You coulda came get me, bro. Afraid I was gonna steal her from you, huh?"

"Nigga, please. She's not mine to steal. Big ol' rock on her hand. All blingin' and shit."

"For real? Then what you doing thinking about her? Something else must have happened. Whaddup with that?"

"Something else happened . . . but I'm not sure what. We had lunch, but it was supposed to be an interview. I never asked her about the ring. I figured it was none of my business. The problem is I can't stop thinking about her."

"You sound like you're sprung and you haven't even smelled it, let alone tapped it. What's she look like?"

"About this tall, light brown, light brown eyes, fine as all hell. Name's Glover."

"Glover? What the fuck kind of name is that? You mean 'Danny Glover'? You crazy about a dude?"

"Fuck you, Smit! It's your set." We traded places, as it was Smitty's turn on the weight bench. He hemmed and hawed and adjusted his waistband before sitting down.

"How you guys wind up going to lunch? And why didn't you tell a brother?"

"She called me. Strangest shit. She pulled my application and called me about some jobs at the DMV."

"Maybe she wanted to give you a *driving* test, *Maxwell*. Haha!"

"I would think it was maybe a coincidence, but I'm not sure. I get this vibe when I'm near her."

"That vibe's called a 'hard-on', nigga. I get that vibe often around women. Trust a player on that. So, did you get the digits?"

"Nah. I don't know if she's even about that. Don't want to make a fool of myself. Everything could be about business. You know I need a job. I don't want to fuck anything up by playing Super-nigga. I leave that shit to you."

"Sounds to me like she's up to something, bro. Be careful you don't get played. Seriously."

"I won't, bro."

"Um, Max?"

"Yeah?"

"Could you get this weight off me?"

27   *Glover*

Wednesday rolled around and I was dead tired after work. I had promised Lionel that I would go by his parents', but I really didn't want to be bothered after fighting the traffic home. A promise was a promise though. I kicked my shoes off and rested my eyes for five minutes before venturing back out. Bel Air was only five miles away, but it was several pocket books away from where I was. The view of the million dollar homes (and their gates) did make for a scenic drive while my little Civic wound through West Sunset Boulevard. I was passing the intersection with Whittier when I saw Mona's dad's car at the corner. I had forgotten that he lived near here. I caught a glimpse of him with the new Mrs. Stevens sitting beside him. Damn. The sister looked to be about my age. They had so much in common, I'm sure. Hope he was getting his money's worth.

I came upon the white walls of the Dunning Estate before I knew it. Lionel told me the estate had been built in the 1930s. For as big as it was, it had an understated elegance about it. Maybe it was the Mediterranean design. Lionel's parents bought the place about ten years ago when they moved from Ladera Heights. Lionel's father was a prominent attorney in L.A. who had recently retired and his mother, Adele, was one of those society types who loved having her name in print. She really must have hated this wedding, but she usually honored her son's wishes.

The gate opened for me when I pulled up. I assumed some-body was watching my car on some security monitor. This was just like something off television. I drove around the half-circle in front of the entrance and parked by the water fountain. I was careful not to scratch their Mercedes that was parked in front, while I drove past it. I really wanted to put on some sweats after work, but chose to stay in my work attire. Might as well not give Adele anything else to talk about.

I was greeted at the door by this demure, little Spanish woman who walked me through the foyer and past the double stairwell. There was a canvas portrait of the Dunning family on the wall above the left stairwell, which I glanced at. I wondered sarcastically if they were planning on having another painting done to add me. I was escorted toward the back of the first floor and down a hall. The light disoriented me as I walked out into an enormous open room lined with an entire wall of glass. The sun was pouring in from all around and glistened off the marble floor I walking was on. The glass wall was looking out on a palm-tree-lined pool below. The sun was just starting to go down, but it seemed like it was midday in this part of the house. The room was almost bare save for an antique table and a few chairs, but it was large enough to host a large party. Lionel's mother was standing with her back to us. She was surveying the grounds out back. There was a reason this location was picked for this. This was Adele's turf and she wanted to let me know it too. A grand scale and I was just a little pebble in her eyes. A pebble that happened to be marrying her dear son though.

"Aww! Glover! How are you my dear?" Adele turned as if we had startled her. Adele was a virtual dead ringer for Eartha Kitt in the face, but wore her hair in a short salt and pepper Afro. She stood before me in an embroidered multi-colored tu-nic with gold sandals. We walked toward each other and gave a gentle embrace followed by the complimentary kiss on the cheek.

Adele then held my face in her hands and stared at me with an adoring smile.

"Oh, Glover I'm glad you made it." She then turned briefly to my escort and said, "That will be all, Rosa." With that Rosa smiled and disappeared back up the hallway from whence she came.

"How are you, Mrs. Dunning?"

"I'm fine, Glover. Please. Call me mother . . . or at least 'Adele'. I hope you will come to think of me as that over time. I know I could never replace your dearly departed mother and I would never presume otherwise. I just want you to know that I am here for you."

"Thank you. How is Mr. Dunning?"

"He's doing very well, Glover. He's somewhere on the property. Probably outside looking to change the landscaping. He's always trying to stay busy since retiring. Come over here. I have some ideas to run by you." With that, Adele led me over to the antique table.

"I have a couple of sample menus from the caterers as well as some wedding dress samples. We're going to need to get you fitted. You're a size twelve, right?"

"Uh, no. I'm a size ten." Bitch.

"Oh, I'm sorry. I was close though. Do you like Vera Wang's designs or Escada? I see a lot of that these days."

"I *love* Vera Wang. I just wish I could afford her stuff."

"Nonsense, child. Vera Wang it is. When do you want to be fitted? We don't have time to waste and I'm already going to pay extra due to the late notice."

"I don't know. As soon as possible, I guess. Do you have to call the store?"

"Store? No, dear. I'm going to call *her*. Your dress is going to be an original. I can't have my son's bride in anything less." Adele then let out a chuckle.

"Oh. That's really okay. A store-bought dress is expensive enough, but an original? I can't pay that kind of money back. "

Adele ignored my comments and continued, "I'll need a list of guests for the invitations. We'll also need to get your bridesmaid and matron of honor fitted. I also have two locations on standby down in Catalina. Are you positive about getting married there? There are some really beautiful sites up the coast and Catalina is so, so . . . I don't know . . . "

"I'm sure about Catalina, Mrs. Dunning. If you don't like the location then don't worry about it. I can take care of it by myself."

"No, dear. I don't have any problems with your choice. I'm just trying to help you explore your options. That's all. Tell me, do you like pate'?"

We explored my "options" for another hour. I had to be to work the next day so I used that excuse to end the agony. I hated having to come back. I jumped in my Civic and sped away back down West Sunset. I had left my cell phone on the seat. I picked it up to call Lionel. I'm sure he wanted to hear how I made out with his mother. I had pressed the first two digits when I came to a red light. I stared into the light for a few seconds before hitting the "clear" button. I then reached into my purse for a folded piece of paper and started dialing again.

"Hello?"

"Did I wake you up?"

"Umm, nah." He was lying. "What's up?"

"What are you doing tomorrow?"

" . . . Nothing."

"How about dinner this time? On me."

28   *Max*

I was surprised by the call in the middle of the night. I was even more surprised by the voice on the other end and the invitation. She actually trusted me in her apartment. I was scheduled to work Thursday night since Samir had taken me off the weekend schedule due to the barbecue. I managed to beg my way off Thursday's schedule, as I couldn't pass up this opportunity to see Glover again. I owed Samir big time.

When I was given directions, I discovered that Glover stayed on the same end of town. When I first moved out here, I had even considered moving into the apartments where she stayed. They were just a little bit pricier than what I had in mind. Her directions were perfect anyway. I found a parking spot next to her car and drove right in.

On the way there, I had picked up a bottle of Zinfandel and a single yellow rose from the Lucky on South Sepulveda. That was after I got a haircut that I really didn't need. Wasn't sure what I was walking into, but I didn't want to go there looking sloppy. When the door opened, I realized my decision was the right one. I stood there in the hall and checked out Glover who was looking all good and shit. She was casually dressed in a yellow outfit with some black slip-on sandals. The pants were those that stop just below the knee and the top was a short sleeve pullover. I caught a glimpse of a black undershirt strap by her shoulder. Glover had a small gold chain draped on her neck. It was just below that pretty face of hers. Her lips were covered in lipstick that I was just dying to sample . . . right off of them of course. She was cutting those eyes at me and smirking.

She leaned against the open door and said, "Well, are you going to come in or are you going to just stand there staring?"

"Both options seem pretty good to me at this point, but I think I'll come in." I strolled in past Glover to allow her to close the door. As she closed the door, I stole a glance at her backside. The snugness of her pants made it easy. The things women wore for us men. When she turned back around to welcome me, I leaned over and gave a short, platonic hug and kiss on the cheek. Damn. I caught a whiff of her perfume. Women placed that shit in all the right places to drive a brother crazy.

"Welcome to mi casa, *Señor* Guillory. You didn't have any problems with my directions, huh?"

"No. Not at all. I've actually been here before. When I was apartment hunting. Oh. This is for you." I handed the yellow rose to her. I hadn't planned on it matching her outfit.

"Aww! That's so sweeeet! Thank you!" Glover then walked closer and placed her right hand over my shoulder where it came to rest around the back of my neck. She then slowly, gracefully pulled herself up toward me and planted a soft kiss on my cheek. Her lips lingered there for a moment before she lowered herself away from me.

"Oh, you brought wine too? Let me take that off your hands." She then sashayed off into her kitchen with the wine in hand. "Make yourself comfortable. Dinner will be ready in a minute."

"Can I take my shoes off then?"

"Haha. Sure. Just don't funk up my apartment."

I was about to sit down on her couch when I noticed some pictures by her television set. One of the photos was of Glover as a child at the beach. She was with a woman who I presumed was her mother. Another was Glover in a graduation gown. The same woman was with her in the photo.

"Is this your mom in these photos?"

"Yeah. That's my mommy. Those are some of my happy times."

"You were adorable in your little swimsuit. The other picture is of your high school graduation?"

"Yep. That was the last picture of my mother . . . before she passed away. We were like best friends."

"Hearing you say that makes me think about my mother. We're close, but it kinda makes you think. I guess I take tomorrow for granted sometimes."

"Yep. Tomorrow's never promised. Food's ready. I hope you like pasta. You can put on some music while you're over there," Glover said while carrying things out to the table.

I found one of Glover's light jazz CDs and inserted it into the CD player. Glover was back in the kitchen wrestling with the bottle opener and the Zinfandel. She had obviously gone to great lengths to prepare the meal. Fresh salad, fettuccini Alfredo with shrimp, and hot buttered garlic bread. I didn't know if my wine was the right one for the dish, but Glover didn't complain. Over the small talk of dinner, the bottle dwindled down quickly. I should have picked up two bottles instead. The wine loosened me up enough to begin really speaking my mind.

"Glover, what's going on? Really. I see the rock on your hand, but I'm feeling something else. Would you help a brother out?"

"Haha. Alright. I'll come clean. I intentionally pulled your application and called you. This is not the normal kind of shit that I do, you understand. I'm acting completely out of character. I'm usually a straightforward woman."

"So be one now." I decided to press the issue.

"Okay. I'll spit it all out. I'm feeling you, but I think you know that already. I'm also engaged . . . to a wonderful man. That means we could never be anything more than friends. I barely know you, but I feel so comfortable when I'm around you. I should have been straight up with you from the beginning instead of acting like a scheming tackhead. I'm sorry, Max."

"I'm alright. At least we've got that in the open. What's his name?"

"Lionel."

"Lionel must be doing pretty good for himself. He's got you and he's able to afford a ring like that. Yep. He's very lucky."

"Are you upset with me, Max? You have every right to be. I would understand it if you walked out and never talked to me again."

"Okay. It's my turn to come clean. I saw the ring when I first met you. I was hoping it was just for show or to keep the brothers off your back. You have been on my mind ever since I first met you. At least now I know where we stand. I can live with that. Hell, I have no choice actually."

"Again, I'm sorry, Max. I know I'm wrong for what I'm about to say, but I would still like to get to know you better . . . as a friend. Would you be okay with that?"

"Yeah. I would like that Glover. I don't have that many friends out here and one can never have enough friends. Shake on it?"

I stuck my hand out across the table and Glover took it. Our eyes met in understanding. God, she was so beautiful and had brains to go along with it. Lionel was definitely a lucky man.

"Max?"

"Yeah?"

"You didn't get the DMV job. They hired someone else. I found out late this afternoon. I did forward your info to them like I promised."

"I knew you did. No matter what else, I trusted you. Thanks for trying though."

"Would you like some ice cream for dessert?"

If I could eat it off you. "Umm . . . sure."

"It's Cookies n' Cream. Is that okay?"

"Yep."

"*Good*. It's in my freezer. The bowls are in the cabinet on the left and the spoons are in the second drawer. Bring me some too."

"You've got a lot of nerve Glover," I said dryly as I got up and walked past her and into the kitchen. Everything was where she said it would be and we sat around the table trading jokes while eating dessert.

Shortly after dessert, Glover's phone rang. I could tell it was one of her girlfriends and I chose that time to make my exit even though she only talked briefly. Glover walked me to the door and we gave each other a brief hug. The atmosphere was different from when I first entered her apartment.

"Did you pick up that Oriental rug at the swap meet?" I said while pointing back toward her sofa.

"It's a *Persian* rug and 'yes' I did buy it there. How did you know?"

"My neighbor, Smitty, has the same one in his apartment," I said with a smile. "Speaking of him, we're barbecuing this Saturday. We'll be out by the pool and stuff. You're welcome to come."

"Aww! Thank you. I'd love to come."

"*Good*. It's at my apartment. I would give you the address and stuff, but I'm sure you already have that from my application. Goodnight." With that said, I turned and strolled off. I loved getting back at her for the ice cream thing.

"Good night to you too, smart ass," I heard Glover laughingly say as she closed her door.

The walk to my car was filled with thoughts of the interesting night with Ms. Glover. I walked out from the stairwell and toward the parking lot while whistling. I was caught up in thought and didn't see the dark colored Volvo that almost hit me as it sped by. It was going pretty fast for an apartment complex parking lot. Probably a drunk.

29 *Glover*

I didn't intend on rushing Mona off the phone when she called that night, but Max was about to leave. I would see Mona the next day anyway. When I told Mona that I had company, she assumed it was Lionel. I didn't tell her otherwise.

Even though I had two late evenings in a row with my future mother-in-law and Max, I had a spring in my step by the end of the week. It was a busy Friday and I spent a lot of it on the phone with Adele doing wedding planning and scheduling. It was becoming apparent that the last minute planning would begin to take even more of my time than my job itself. Lionel's request to leave this job was beginning to seem more inviting.

I ended my Friday differently this time. I put off the evening with my girls and decided to go it alone. I went jogging around the block several times with my Walkman for company. I stopped when I figured I had gone three miles. It had been months as my winded breathing was reminding me. Upon my return, I ate some leftover fettuccini from the night before and drew a relaxing bath for myself. I soaked in the bath oil while surrounded by lavender scented candles. The Isley Brothers Greatest Hits put me in a trance and I wound up falling asleep. When I woke up, the candles were still lit, but my water was cool.

I slept in late Saturday morning. I had some soreness setting in from my jog and decided to try to wait it out. It also felt good to lay under my comforter and not think about anything. The morning rolled by and I started to stir. I reached my hand out from under the comforter and picked up my telephone from its stand. I dialed the number off the piece of paper.

"Hello?"

"Hey. It's me."

"Oh, don't tell me you're calling to bail on me!"

"No. No. I was calling to see if you're really okay with me going by there."

"Of course I'm okay with it. I wouldn't have asked you. Friends, right?"

"Right."

"Then hurry up and bring yo ass over here! Feel free to bring the rest of you too. We're about to start cueing."

"Haha. Alright. I'm coming."

"That's what I'm talkin' about! Before I forget . . . don't forget your swimsuit. My apartment may not be as posh as yours, but we have a pool too."

"I'll think about it, Max."

"My apartment number is 105. My white Celica is parked directly outside. If I'm not inside, I'll be out by the pool. Alright?"

"Alright. See you soon."

I hung up the phone and climbed out of bed. I got in a good long cat-like stretch before walking over to my dresser. What to wear?

I didn't know how anyone else was going to be dressed and I spent twenty minutes in front of the mirror like a silly school-girl. I finally selected my outfit and laid it out on the bed. I also found a swimsuit. I packed my navy blue one piece Anne Cole with the white mesh midsection in my tote bag along with my cell phone. Afterwards, I skipped into the bathroom to get my act together.

I arrived at Max's complex two hours later and stepped out of my car. While looking for them, I passed the blue and white apartments and had to double back up Venice. I was wearing my white linen shorts, my white Club Monaco tube top with Navy stripes, and my white canvas tennis shoes for the old feet. My tortoise shades were keeping the sun out of my eyes and I had my tote bag draped over my shoulder. Might as well go in coordinated. There were two units close to where Max's car was parked. One was on the second floor and the other was just below it. Both of their patio doors were slightly open and I could hear music coming from both. I figured that Max's was the ground level unit based on his apartment number.

I walked through the hallway to the interior of the complex and located Max's front door. I had correctly guessed the right unit. I took a deep breath and knocked on the door. No answer. Maybe the music was too loud. I waited then knocked harder. A heavyset man answered the door with a smile.

"Hello. I must have the wrong apartment."

"Oh! You must be looking for Max! He's by the pool with the food. C'mon, I'll walk you there. He's been expecting you." The brother sure was the friendly sort. I was wondering exactly what Max had told him about me.

"By the way, pleased to meet you. Samir." His large hand engulfed mine.

"Glover. Do you live here too, Samir?"

"No. I live over in Gardena. I'm Max's manager over at Denny's. He's a good worker. Yep. My boy's gonna blow up one day. Soon. Just you wait and see." His smile revealed an almost fatherly pride in Max.

He walked me out in the courtyard. Max was standing by the barbecue pit next to the pool. I finally got a good view of his shoulders due to the black muscle shirt the brother was sporting. Max was clad all in black; Adidas pants with the white stripes down the sides with the tennis shoes to match. A small group of people was standing near Max and were talking and joking.

Max saw me and came running up. He put his arms around me and gave a tight squeeze. His attention made me feel good. Max said enthusiastically, "Hey, lady! You made it, huh?"

I replied, "I said I was coming, right?"

"Damn!" I heard from behind Max. It was one of his friends I assumed. He was a little skinny fella in a pair of blue jeans and a FUBU shirt. A heavy sister with a lollipop in her mouth gave the little dude a massive elbow, presumably in response to his outburst. The sister then turned her attention back to me and cut a nasty look with her beady eyes.

I thought to myself, "Lord, don't let there be some shit up in here."

"Glover, let me introduce you to some people. This is my boy, Smitty." This guy was actually shorter than me. Nice enough though. I could tell he was a character. A male version of Charmaine. He was quick to shake my hand in a very safe manner. I bet his chest was red from the elbow he got.

"This is his girl, Zena." Warrior princess, she wasn't. She smiled, but her beady eyes didn't look any happier than before.

"This is Zena's sister, Sonia." She was a smaller version of the Lollipop Kid and had been lurking in the background. She was cuter than her sister, but had a dead serious look on her face. Not even a fake smile. She was making it apparent that I was unwelcome here. Shit. Like I really cared.

There were a few other small groups of people carrying on with their own conversations. I assumed they lived in the apartments too as they would come and go from the pool area. A boom box was resting on one of the patio tables next to the aluminum pans filled with barbecued sausage, hamburgers, ribs, and kabobs. I wasn't that hungry as I came primarily to hang, but the food was lookin' good.

"You're looking good as always, Glover. Excuse my smell. I'm smelling like smoke right about now."

"I don't mind, Max. You're the chef today, so I'll forgive you. Do you have somewhere I can put my tote bag?"

"Yeah. My apartment's open. People have been going in and out of there, so you may want to put it up in the bedroom. Samir walked you from there, right?"

"Yeah. He's a nice person. Thinks very highly of you, Mr. Guillory. I guess I kinda do too."

Max blushed slightly and we exchanged a glance. I tilted my head so my eyes could meet his. Max stood there silent with a bottle of barbecue sauce in his hand.

At that moment, one of the fellow partygoers broke our brief moment with, "Hey, Max! That's your girlfriend, dawg?"

Max snapped out of it and looked toward the brother. Max replied, "Nah dawg, she's not mine. She's just a . . . a friend of mine." Max had paused as he looked back at me and saw my bare left hand. He was thrown for a loop in mid-sentence and his eyes widened. He looked up from my hand and saw my smile. I hadn't planned on leaving my ring off. It just worked out that way. I accidentally left it on my dresser when I was trying on clothes in front of my mirror. I was halfway to Max's place when I realized it wasn't on my hand. I almost turned around, but decided it didn't really matter at this moment. Max's confusion was actually cute.

I said, "I'll be back. I'm going put up my bag" and left toward Max's apartment.

"Hurry back. Don't make me come looking for you."

"What if that's what I want?" I looked over my shoulder and cut another smile at Max. I loved playing around like that, but somewhere beneath my words I felt that maybe I was serious. I had to get a grip. Zena and Sonia's eyes were on me and I could see them whispering out the corners of my eyes.

Max's apartment had the look of a college student's, albeit a lot neater. I located the bedroom and placed my tote bag on the side of Max's bed where it wouldn't be too visible. The bedroom was immaculate. Not what I expected. There was still a lot to learn about, Max. I ran my hand across the top of his bed and walked over to his oak dresser.

Sitting on his dresser beside his Mason ring was a framed picture. It was of Max and his mom. A picture taken at his college graduation apparently. I was startled by sounds in the living room. Somebody had entered the apartment. I walked out of Max's bedroom.

"Well if it isn't Ms. Siddity. Look at this, Sonia." The Lollipop Kid and sis had some shit on their collective mind. I tried to ignore them as I walked by.

Sonia mumbled, "Who the fuck does she think she is? Sorry ass bitch."

"*Excuse me?* I couldn't help but overhear you talking about a sorry ass bitch. Someone I know?" I was about to get "ig'nit" with the heavyweight tag team and possibly get drove by them, but the sista wasn't backing down. That lollipop was going straight down Zena's throat with the help of my little fist.

"Girl, you steppin' to Max like that and disrespectin' my little sister. We don't play that shit. Maybe that's cool where you from, but not around here."

"Oh! So Max is *your* man?" I looked toward Sonia with a crazy smile and half-laugh that caught her off guard. I could tell she was about to lie by the way she paused and looked away. I learned to look for that in my job.

"Oh there you two are! I can't take you two anywhere. All frowned up like Menace II Society number one and two." It was Max's friend, Smitty. "I need to make another beer run. You wanna drive me, Zena? You know you're almost out of lollipops, baby."

Zena and Sonia loosened up and stormed out of the apartment. As they walked out, they gave me parting looks and Sonia motioned with her hand like a gun to her head and went "poof".

Smitty started to walk out behind them, but stopped and said, "Sorry about them. They're all talk . . . most of the time. Zena called herself hooking up Sonia with Max, but Max wasn't havin' that anyway. I guess Zena won't be giving me any tonight. Damn. You know you got my boy goin' crazy, right? Be gentle though. He don't get it that often and you . . . you foin as *hell*. Girl, you damn lucky I'm with Zena today."

"No, no. We're *just* friends. I'm engaged and . . . "

"Riiiiiiiiiiight! I saw how you two look at each other. Don't shit a shitter. See ya later." Smitty then shot out the door to catch up with the two headbusters. He enjoyed making me squirm.

I let out a huge sigh before heading out the door. I didn't know what I was getting into when I came here. I was definitely hungry now.

30

Max

I had invited Jay to the barbecue, but he was a "no show". Probably out scheming. It didn't really matter. I had other concerns on my mind. Glover had been gone for awhile and hadn't returned from my apartment. Was she serious about wanting me to come looking for her? Nah. I learned to stop fantasizing when she broke it down to me. No need get my hormones riled up. Just then, Glover walked out into the courtyard. Her shades were off so I was able to look into her pretty brown eyes once again.

"Is everything okay? I was beginning to worry."

"Everything's fine, Max. Thanks for your concern though."

"I fixed a plate for you over there," I said motioning to one of the nearby patio tables.

"You not gonna join me? What kind of host are you anyway?"

"Okay. I'm finished cueing anyway. I'll fix a plate and be right over."

Glover walked over to the table to where her plate was waiting. I relieved myself from my duties at the pit and joined her.

"Did you have any other plans this weekend?"

"No, not really. I cleared my entire schedule just to come here. I had to taste your barbecue."

"Well? What's the verdict?"

"It's good. Share your secret?"

"Beer."

"Beer?"

"Yep. Beer. I pour it over the meat while it's cooking. Just before I dab the sauce on."

"I should have known. You're an alcoholic. Probably full right now."

"Haha. Cute. I don't hear you complaining about the food."

"You know I'm just fucking with you, right?"

"Yeah. I know. You've got some sauce on your face."

"I do? Where?"

"You know I'm just fucking with you, right?"

"Max?"

"Huh?"

"Stop."

"Okay. Glover, what do you like to do for fun? I mean, besides giving people a hard time and making them squirm."

"Heh. You're cute. I like to just listen to music sometimes. I like to travel when I can. I like hanging with my friends most of all. They're important to me."

"Sounds a lot like me. I used to be a party person. Now I'm content to just hang out. Guess I'm either getting old or maybe it's just my priorities changing. I guess a move to a city like Los Angeles will do that to you as well. It has been an adjustment."

"What? The hustle and bustle?"

"Not really that as much as the unfamiliarity of it all. I was on familiar turf back home in Louisiana. The place wasn't that big, so you got a feel for things and people fairly quickly. Here, I'm a little slower to trust. There's so much that is not as it seems, y'know?"

"Me included, huh?" Glover said as she rested her hand under her chin.

"Oh, no! I wasn't including you in that statement. This is a place where so many people come to reinvent themselves. Fresh starts. I guess I'm included in that group."

"So, what do you want to change, Max? Better yet, what *would* you change in your life right now?"

"Well, I would have my career on a roll. Whatever it is. A nice house with an ocean view and someone special to share it with. I've got you in my life and that's something I wouldn't change. Even if it is just as a friend." I got on a roll and let that slip out.

"Sometimes friendship is the most important thing, Max. Trust me on that."

"Did you bring your swimsuit?"

"That's for me to know and you to find out."

I playfully said, "Hey! Nudity is cool too. The pool is heated, but you still might be a tad cold."

"Always the joker. Are you ever serious?"

"Most of the time. I just like seeing the life in your face when you smile."

"You're the one with the nice smile, Mr. Guillory."

The mutual admiration society continued its meeting for the next hour and was only interrupted briefly as partygoers moved on. Smitty had returned from his beer run and was keeping an angry Zena and Sonia at bay. He then moved the remainder of the party upstairs to his place. The sun was starting to set in the West and some clouds began rolling in.

"Do you want to go up to Smitty's? It's up to you."

"No, not really." Glover had pushed her chair back from the table and was walking around the courtyard area lazily. She had picked up a wine cooler from the ice chest. "Is that a Jacuzzi on the other end of the pool?"

"Yep. It's actually working this week. I knock these apartments, but they're really pretty nice. I wish they had a gym though. Even a small one."

"You could come by and use mine sometime, Max. Don't want you losing that muscle tone, now do we?"

"That's a no-no. Friends aren't supposed to talk about each other's bodies. Not even if they're as fine as yours." Glover looked back and smiled. She then approached me and took my arm in hers.

"C'mon! Show me your place before we come back down here. I need to change anyway."

"Oh! So you did bring a suit!"

We walked to my apartment where I gave her an informal tour of my tiny place. I sat on the arm of my sofa while Glover looked through my photo album. She took great delight in laughing at photos of my developmental years filled with bad clothing ideas that we all thought were "da bomb" at the time.

"I need to shower before we head down to the pool. I smell just like that pit down there. Make yourself comfortable and remember to tell any females that you're my cousin if they call. Okay?"

"Yes, sir! Any other orders? Shall I wash dishes or anything?"

"No, that'll do, madam. You know you can hang upstairs if you want while I shower. I won't be long." I pointed up at the ceiling as we could hear the muffled sounds of music and conversation up above.

"Nah. I'm not really up for seeing *certain* people. I'm here to have fun and the company down here is just fine."

"Oh. Glover, did something happen with Zena or Sonia? They didn't try to start any shit, huh?"

"Nothing I couldn't handle. They were just being catty in their own special way. I'm not causing any problems with you and Sonia, am I? Please tell me. I don't want to assume I know the answer."

"*Sonia*!? Nah! Zena calls herself trying to set me up with her crazy sister, but she knows I'm not interested. You're cool. Trust me. There is nothing going on there and never will be. So you're gonna sit tight?"

"Yep. Get your ass in there and shower before I change my mind. You know a sister doesn't want to get her hair wet anyway."

"Alright! Alright!"

I walked into my bedroom and tossed my smoky smelling clothes in the dirty clothes hamper. A cold shower would be a good idea, but I needed this shower primarily to get clean this time. I didn't want to leave Glover all alone, so I soaped up quickly. My bathroom door was partially open, so I yelled out to Glover that I would be out soon. She responded, but sounded much closer than the living room. It was probably my imagination. As I turned the water off, I reached for my towel to wipe the water from my eyes. I heard rustling sounds coming from my bedroom. It was Glover. Through the crack in my door, I could see that she was changing into her swimsuit. As I dried off, I felt like a perv. I still couldn't take my eyes off her. She had to have heard the water stop and would be expecting me to walk out eventually. My eyes followed every inch of her from her shoulders to her hips as her top came off followed by her shorts.

"Told you I wouldn't be long," I shouted from inside the bathroom. I felt wrong without giving her a warning.

"Hope you don't mind. I left my bag in here and started changing." She didn't speed up her pace or anything. She slowly reached for the clasp on the front of her bra and let it drop to the floor. Her bare breasts were exposed and I started stirring as I saw her lovely brown, erect nipples. She had to know that I could see her every move.

"That's okay. You had to change somewhere . . . and I'm in here hogging the bathroom. Haha." Her panties dropped to the floor next. I had a perfectly naked woman in my bedroom and my every instinct was to rush out there and take her in my arms. I wanted to make love to her sooo bad. No. She was for someone else. My swim trunks were in there with her. I decided to wait until she was dressed before going out there. Besides, I had a serious hard-on and I don't think my towel would have kept her from noticing. She had to have noticed the crack in the door, but I wasn't going to ask. I was feeling guilty on one hand, but enjoyed it on the other.

When I knew Glover was decent, I made my exit from the bathroom. I had my towel around me, but was still a little wet. No sense in drying off completely if you're about to jump in a pool. Glover was standing at the side of my bed and was looking as good in her swimsuit as she was while briefly naked. She was wearing a dark blue one piece off one shoulder. It had a white mesh area that showed off her flat stomach. She didn't have a TLC six-pack, but it was nothing to sneeze at. I politely smiled and walked over to my dresser. In my mirror, I saw her behind me. She was folding her clothes on my bed, but was slyly checking me out. I found my black swim trunks in the middle drawer and pulled them out to put on. Glover excused herself from my bedroom, but had to pass by me on the way out.

As she walked into the living room, she joked, "Do you want me to leave a crack in the door?" Glover was fire. I was already sweating from the heat.

I exited the bedroom and we grabbed some drinks. Glover grabbed a peach cooler to head down to the pool with, while I grabbed a longneck. It was getting dark and the outdoor lights would be coming on shortly. We had been up in my apartment longer than I expected, as Smitty had already moved the barbecue pit and cleaned up at pool side. I owed him. We placed the coolers on the ground near the edge of the pool. Glover slowly lowered herself into the pool as I held her right hand. When she was completely in, she began backstroking toward the far end.

"Max, you know you owe me for another relaxer. You're the one who talked me into this. This chlorine's kickin'. Denny's pay you enough to take care of my next hair appointment?"

I followed in Glover's wake so my head was visible right by her feet as she paddled.

I replied, "Glover, I would say 'fuck you' for that Denny's crack, but you might take it literally, Ms. Soon-To-Be-Married. We can't have you trying to freak me in the pool. I don't swim that well."

Glover then took her feet and kicked a wave up in my face. I dove below after I cleared my eyes and came up below her. She playfully screamed as I picked her up and dumped her. We wrestled around in the water for a minute until we wound up face to face in each other's arms.

The laughter slowly died down as our eyes locked on each other. Our wet bodies were pressed up against each other and started pressing harder. Glover's hands were trembling as she pulled me against her. My hands were sliding against the small of her back. We were heading somewhere we had been fighting. She seemed like she was in great pain and I just wanted to make it all better. I put my finger under her chin and lifted her head up. There was great confusion in her eyes. It seemed like part of her wanted to run off, while the other part wanted something else. Me. I leaned over to finally kiss those lips . . .

Bloop! A large raindrop fell onto my nose. I flinched in surprise. It was enough to break the mood that was going down. Several others followed the first drop. Cold rain.

Glover relaxed her grip on me. Her head lowered and she whispered under her breath,
"God's crying." It was barely audible.

"What did you say?" The rain was starting to pick up. A freak storm I guess. And they say it never rains in southern California.

"God's crying. My mom used to tell me that when it rained. She used to say that somebody was doing wrong somewhere. Some stuff she brought from Virginia."

"Oh. I see. Let's go in before we catch pneumonia."

We went back inside my apartment. I gave Glover a towel to dry off with and one of my shirts to put on. We were back in friend mode. The way it should be. I grabbed my throw from out of the closet and tossed it to Glover on the couch. She found one of those classic movie channels on TV. I microwaved some popcorn and put it in a bowl for us then joined Glover. She looked exhausted. Emotions can drain you, especially if they catch you off guard.

"Thank you," she said as she took a handful of popcorn out of the bowl. She then leaned against me and put her feet up. I reached over and turned the lights off.

To Sir, With Love had just started on TV. One of my favorites and I hadn't seen it since I was in middle school. Sidney Portier was just introducing himself to the class of crazy British kids. I made it all the way through until the part where the girl in class sang the title song. I was trying to remember her real name, as my eyes became heavy. Glover was already snoring. We fell asleep on the couch that night.

31 *Glover*

It came in slow at first . . . guitars. Then horns? Bump . . . bump, bump, bump. Bump . . . bump, bump, bump. What was Isaac Hayes doing talking in my dreams? I opened one eye and was startled. I wasn't dreaming. It was morning. I was hearing Shaft's theme song. What the fuck was going on? I opened both eyes. I was lying on top of Max on his couch. He was still asleep. My head had been on his chest and he had one arm around me and one hanging down onto the floor. I started looking around to figure out where the music was coming from. The walls were vibrating.

My movement brought Max out of his sleep. He stirred and said, "Good morning, beautiful." That smile of his was showing.

"Hey." I pulled myself closer and just kissed on instinct. No thought. Max was caught off guard, but responded favorably. Our eyes closed and we used our lips to guide each other in sensuous circles. Morning breath was never so good. We continued the kiss as we began to sit upright on the couch. I straddled Max's lap and began pulling his head into my chest. His hands reached up and started unbuttoning my shirt. Correction . . . *his shirt*. And I wanted him to. The only thing wrong was that damn music that was throwing things off. I was just going to ignore it. I started grinding up against his lap and I could feel the morning bulge underneath his shorts. Then it happened.

At first I didn't make it out. But I heard it again. It was a phone. My cell phone. It was in my tote bag and ringing. I blinked my eyes and looked toward Max's bedroom where the ringing was coming from. I had left my tote bag by Max's bed. It was ironic, as I wanted to go to the bedroom, but not to pick up the phone. I looked back down at Max and noticed that he had a serious look on his face. He had brought his hands back down to his side.

"You need to get that, right?"

"Yeah. I guess I do."

Max let out a long breath and turned on his side to face the back of the couch. I ran my hands through my tangled hair and climbed off him. I already knew who it was on the other end of the phone.

"Hello?"

"Hey, baby! Where you been? I've been trying to reach you since yesterday."

"Oh. I've been hanging out with . . . Mona. I . . . I had to do some shopping earlier yesterday. Looking around for things to put on the gift registry too." I hated lying.

"And here I thought you were looking for your honeymoon outfit. Damn. I miss you."

"I miss you too, Lionel."

"Where are you anyway?"

"Um . . . I'm out running errands."

"Sure is quiet. You're in the store?"

"No. I'm in the post office. I was about to pick up some stamps from the machine. I was . . . looking for change when you called."

"Oh. Will I see you today?"

"Yeah. Well, let me get off this phone. The battery's getting low."

"Alright, baby."

"Bye."

I turned back around to see Max leaning in the doorway to his bedroom. If we were both in here a minute ago, we would have been in deep. Very deep.

"Damn girl. That was a pretty impressive story you just told. Lionel, huh?"

"Did you even have to ask."

"No. Just wanted to confirm it though. That 'post office' thing came pretty quickly. Almost like you're used to doing this." I didn't like the tone of his voice when he said that.

"Max, I'm speaking with my fiancé on the phone. How in the *hell* do I explain that I'm at another man's place, wearing another man's shirt, that I spent the night with him, *and* that I was about to have sex with him when he called and interrupted?"

"I thought it would have been more than just 'sex' between us." Max's voice ringed with hurt.

"Oh, stop that! Max, you know what I'm saying. I would apologize for what I started on the couch, but I'm tired of doing that. I meant to do it. I wanted to kiss you and I did."

"It was a good kiss too. It was going a lot further than that and you know it. I guess it was meant for the phone to ring. If we ever go there again, I want you to be mine and mine alone."

"I understand, Max. I think I'll put my clothes on now."

"I'll be in the other room," Max said as he began to close the bedroom door for me.

"Max?"

"Huh?"

"Who in the hell was playing Shaft this early in the morning?!!"

"Heh. That was Smitty. Remind me to tell you about that on our next date."

"What?"

"That was Smitty."

"No! No! The other thing you said!"

"About the date? Oh. Well, I kinda counted this as our first date. After all, I *did* spring for the popcorn last night. You're not keeping my shirt though."

The smart-ass was right though. Max and I saw each other several times over the next few weeks. We would sneak in a lunch here and there or grab some fast food. We even held hands once while taking in a movie. I was leading a secret life. Here I was, the bride-to-be having feelings for another man and spending as much time with him as with my future husband. We wrote it off as a complex friendship and were sure to avoid any more situations that would kick our libidos into overdrive. The thought was still there, but once I was married that would be all over. The person I felt the worse about was Lionel. He was a good man and didn't deserve this. I was just too scared to come clean with everything. I was being a chickenshit, while my fiancé was completely oblivious of my relationship/friendship with Max.

32 *Max*

I guess I was deluding myself. Things had come so close to going over the edge with Glover. After she left that Sunday, I put the shirt she borrowed to my face. I wanted to experience her smell one last time and imagine what-if. I wanted her so badly, but that couldn't happen. She was for someone else. I could tell that Glover was used to being her own woman and was very confident. That included making her own decisions. The problem was that her decisions, if acted on, would wind up being destructive for both of us. With all that known, I still chose to see her several times over the following weeks. I was enjoying getting to know this fascinating woman, but I vowed to never let it get any deeper than it already had gone. Time would tell if we would both be strong enough.

Smitty had been at his new job at West-tel for a few weeks now. I kinda missed hanging out with him on weekdays. He had borrowed my car a few times when his hooptie was being uncooperative. Smitty seemed to be getting his life on track and nobody was prouder of my boy than me. I would be glad when I was doing the same. I hadn't heard from Jay much these days. Things were strained ever since that night at Captains.

I was working graveyards and decided to see if Smitty wanted to hang on the weekend. We hadn't thrown the football around at the park in a long time. I called Smitty that Saturday to see what he was doing. He was washing clothes, but would be finished soon.

Smitty was to come get me when he was ready. I heard a knock on my door and figured it was him. I opened the door to a fist in the face.

Blam!

I crumpled to the floor while holding my nose. My eyes were watering, but I could see this bald, dark skinned brother standing over me. I didn't see a gun in his hand. He was all in black and judging by the Rolex on his wrist, he wasn't here to rob me. The look on his face told me it was personal.

"Get up, bitch! I'm about to have some fun with you!"

"Let me guess. Lionel." I was picking myself up off the floor now. My nose was still stinging, but it wasn't broken. It was time to return the favor.

"Good guess, bitch. Who do you think you're fuckin' with? Your broke ass is gonna remember this ass whippin'!"

The "broke" comment really fired me up. I tensed up to lunge at Lionel. Everything was about to get crazy. A large howl came from the hallway behind Lionel. It distracted us both. Lionel began to turn toward the noise, but it was too late. Smitty's little 5'5 ass came flying through the open door like a madman and landed on Lionel's back. The two of them went spinning around as Smitty had one arm around Lionel's neck to choke him, while he used his free hand to punch upside Lionel's head. As they flailed around, I was knocked back down by one of Smitty's legs. The two of them formed a crazy mass of arms and legs and grunts and growls as my pictures crashed to the floor and one of my lamps flew across the room. Shit. I was trying to keep the place presentable.

For what seemed like an eternity, probably less than thirty seconds had passed. The surprise of Smitty's attack had worn off as Lionel reached up and flipped Smitty off him. Right onto my coffee table. Smitty came down with a crash and glass flew up as my table split in half. The move Lionel made was almost a thing of beauty if it wasn't my boy and my place getting destroyed. I was back on my feet again.

"Broke ass nigger, huh?"

I wasn't much of a brawler, but my right had dropped a couple of fools in my time. As Lionel turned toward me, I smiled. I wasn't about to sneak him. I wanted him to see this coming. I put my all into my swing and as my fist shot toward Lionel's head, the strangest thing happened. Lionel's head wasn't there when my fist arrived. In one fluid move, the brother sidestepped my fist and delivered his own punch to my gut. I was getting tired of being knocked down. I dropped to one knee, but still lunged at Lionel. I finally landed a punch on this guy. I didn't plan on catching him in his neck, but it did send him stumbling back into my couch. As I ran toward the couch, I saw Smitty trying to get up off the floor. I gave Smitty a look to stay out of it. The pained look on his face told me Smit was happy to oblige.

I punched Lionel one last time before he kneed me in my gut. The knee knocked what little wind was left right out of me. I was crouched over and we both were out of steam.

Lionel said, "I think you got the message." He then turned to stroll out my door.

Before he was completely out; he reached in his wallet. He took a dollar bill out, balled it up, and threw it over his shoulder as he disappeared. The dollar bill landed in the middle of the floor. The living room looked like a cyclone had hit it. Smitty was sitting up now and was rubbing his back.

"Damn, Max. Was that some Tae-Bo shit he was using? I need go to those classes. He whipped *your* ass with that chop suey shit."

"Fuck you. I thought it was you at the door."

"Well, at least he left a buck to pay for the shit he broke. Nigga can't be all that bad," Smitty said as he let out a chuckle.

I leaned over and snatched the dollar off the floor then walked over to close the apartment door. I unfolded the dollar partially and hurled it down again in disgust.

"Max, was that ol' girl's man?"

"Yeah. I think so, Smit."

"You gonna tell Glover about this, dawg?"

"Nah. She's got enough on her mind. Damn. I feel like I've seen him somewhere else before."

"Maybe he whipped your ass in a different life."

"No, I'm serious. Maybe I saw a picture of him at Glover's. Oh well."

"Max?"

"Yeah, Smit."

"This ain't no dollar he threw. This is a Benjamin. That nigga just threw away a hundred-dollar bill. Daaaamn."

"Fuck him. You want it, Smit?"

"Hell yeah I want it! You don't want to go play football still, huh?"

"Nah."

"Good! I say we go spend that bald mutherfucker's money! We can load up on shit at the swap meet."

33

Glover

A weekend had gone by without hearing from either Lionel or Max. I had called Max once, but decided not to leave a message. He probably was working or doing his own thing. I wasn't his woman, so it was none of my business. That's what I kept telling myself. It was more unusual not to hear from Lionel.

Mona and Charmaine could tell that something other than marriage preparations was going on with me. I had become secretive and preoccupied. Monday would bring with it new developments. Charmaine had come in late and got written up by Mr. Marx. She almost walked out before I calmed her down. Mona was keeping to herself that day, as she didn't want to draw Mr. Marx's attention to her. Mona knew to steer clear when appropriate.

I was returning calls most of the day and following up to update records. As I completed a call, I prepared to check on Lionel. For all I knew, something could have happened to him. I had the button depressed on the phone when it rang.

"Good morning, this is Ms. McDaniel. May I help you?"

"Heh. Don't you mean 'Mrs. Dunning'?"

"Hey, you! I was just about to call you!"

"Yeah. What are you doing?"

"Work. Same old. Same old. I hadn't heard from you. You okay?"

"Yeah, baby. I've just been busy. I need to talk to you . . . about things."

"O . . . okay. When?"

"I'm down the street now."

Lionel showed up at my job five minutes later. He had a nervous demeanor about him and was not wearing his usual weekday business suit. He was wearing shades and had a denim button-down shirt with white shorts. I managed to take an early break and walked out with him onto the parking lot. Lionel wasn't alone. His cousin, Jacob, who was his best man, was sitting inside the Volvo. Jacob looked up when he saw us, gave a quick smile, then looked down to fiddle with Lionel's radio. Jacob knew something I didn't and chose to stay out of it. We leaned on the front of Lionel's car. It was a warm day, but we had some cloud cover.

"You're off today? I didn't know."

"Yeah. I had to get fitted today. I'll be taking a lot more time off as the wedding gets closer. You still want to get married, *right*?"

"Yeah, baby. What's up with that?"

"Nothing. I just feel we have choices we need to make . . . before we're married. Actually, I made my choice when I asked you to marry me. Maybe you have to . . . clear things up." Lionel was avoiding making eye contact as he leaned on the car next to me. He would periodically look over at me when trying to emphasize his point. I caught a glance at a bruise under those shades. I reached toward Lionel's face. He pulled away and gently pulled my hand down.

"Lionel? What happened?"

"It's nothing. I had an accident the other day. No big deal."

"Jacob, what happened?"

Jacob turned his attention to me long enough to shrug, then went back to playing with the radio.

"Lionel, what do you mean by 'choices'?"

"Just what I said, baby. I think that you might have some issues you need to clear up. You have some choices you need to make if our future is going to be as bright as it can be, baby. You seem distant at times, it's hard to catch up with you sometimes, and I know my mother hasn't heard from you in a few weeks. We're running out of time here. I'm just here to give you a 'heads-up'."

Oh my God. He knew about Max. He was virtually coming out and telling me he knew.

I'm sure he saw the shock in my face even though he continued to look down at the parking lot through his shades. I didn't know what to say. He didn't need me to say anything. He wasn't here for a response; he was here to make a statement.

"I have to get back to work, Lionel."

"I know. We gotta roll anyway. I have to check on some other things for the wedding. You know, we never decided on where to honeymoon."

"I don't know, Lionel. Jamaica? Europe? Africa?"

"Let me know when you decide. I don't care as long as I'm there with you. I love you."

I smiled and gave Lionel a hug. I gave him a light kiss before he got back in the car with Jacob and drove off. Lionel's words were with me the rest of the day at work. I needed to talk to someone about this, but not Max. I needed my sister, Mona.

Upon my return to the office, I told Mona that I needed to talk with her. Mona had been curious about what was going on with me and simply nodded her head. Mona had nothing to say about it the rest of the day. At the end of the workday, Mona told me to follow her home. She probably thought I would get emotional about something and didn't want to see me bawling at work.

I followed Mona to Santa Monica. On the drive west, I had many second thoughts, but erased them from my mind. Mona was my best friend and I felt guilty for shutting her out this whole time. Mona was far from perfect, but she never felt she had to hide things from me. Of course she had her diva persona, but that was usually reserved for others or when in public. The same happy doorman greeted us in the lobby of Mona's condominium. I wondered if he was replaced whenever he got sick.

As Mona unlocked her door, she looked back and casually said, "Did you sleep with him?"

"What?!"

"Did you sleep with him? The cute, creepy guy you've been hanging with in 'secret'."

"Hey! He's not creepy." Damn. Mona figured it out and then had the nerve to insult him.

Mona laughed, "Touched a nerve, huh? Relax I'm just messing with you. He was just so nervous when I saw him at work that time. Whooo! So you did sleep with him."

"No! I didn't sleep with him."

Mona muttered in fake disgust, "Sheesh. I knew you didn't have it in you. You hungry?"

"No. I'm alright. Lionel knows . . . I think."

"Oh. That's bad," Mona said in an understated way. She then walked in her room to drop her purse off.

"Lionel gave me a 'chance' to make up my mind when he came by the office. He didn't sound very happy."

"Would you be? Well, I don't see why he's that upset. It's not like you slept with whatshisname. What *is* his name anyway?"

"His name is Max. Maxwell actually. He's from Louisiana."

"Ooo. Trying to get a bit of 'southern hospitality', huh?"

"*Anyway*. I've been fucking up. I didn't sleep with him, but it's not like I didn't want to. He does something to me. It's different from when I'm with Lionel."

"You sure you're not just running from your upcoming commitment? Heh. I'm familiar with that. Maybe he's just an excuse to avoid thinking about your marriage. You've always avoided the marriage issue with Lionel."

"I . . . I don't think so, Mona. I can't be sure though. How did you know what was going on?"

"It was easy. The way you've been acting at work gave it away. You've been like that since that day we saw you in front of the office with whatshisname. Charmaine thinks he's hot, but she wouldn't tell you that."

"So, you guys have been talking about me, huh? I guess I deserve it though."

"Don't sweat it, Glover. Looks like it's come time to make some choices. I doubt Lionel would understand your 'friendship' with . . . ."

"*Max*. Got it? You're right, Mona. I think something might have happened with him and Lionel."

"Like what?"

34 *Max*

I should have called Samir before popping up on his doorstep that Monday. I had some issues regarding the whole Glover situation and needed someone with wisdom to hear me out. Smitty bummed a ride off of me earlier in the day and I had to be to work that evening. I decided to stop off in Gardena on my way to Denny's.

Samir lived in a modest, single story house that he and his family were renting. Samir's wife, Yvette, was a legal secretary for one of those sleazy TV ambulance chasers. Samir used to tell me stories from his wife's job that would have us cracking up. Samir met Yvette at Denny's before he made manager. Yvette came in one day when her car broke down across the street. Samir told me that he saw her and her two daughters, Asia and Sage, and fell in love with all of them. Of course, he didn't know if their daddy was in the picture at the time. Samir and Yvette started seeing each other and were married six months later. Samir's son, Shaun, came along a year later.

I had only been by Samir's once, but I knew I was at the right place when I saw the kids outside. The two little princesses, Asia and Sage, were standing around lil' Shaun and were kissing on him. Lil' Shaun was wiping his face and trying to get away. When he gets older, I'm sure he won't mind having girls kiss on him. I stepped out my Celica and hit my alarm. The kids jumped at the sound and I had to let out a laugh.

"I know you! You work with my daddy!" Asia screamed out as I stepped onto the porch.

Samir must have heard the noise outside. He came to the door just as I was about to ring.

He opened the storm door with a groan.

"Oh no. Don't tell me. You've come to tell me you quit?"

"No! No! Not yet anyway."

"Whew! You caught me off guard. I was thinking the worst."

"You know I wouldn't just up and leave you like that. You've been too good to me. Besides, I wouldn't be showing up here in my uniform if that was the case."

"You've got a point. Come in, boy." Samir opened the door and was back to grinning. He led me to the living room. I sat down in the oversize leather chair while Samir sat on the end of the love seat across from me.

Samir looked in the direction of the kitchen, "Hey Yvette! Max is here! Can you get us a couple of Budweisers!" I heard Yvette grunt an acknowledgment from the kitchen. It sounded like she was washing something.

"That's okay, man. I'm about to go into work anyway."

"I don't want to hear that, Max. You're a guest in my house. One brew ain't gonna do anything to you anyway."

"Alright."

"Something wrong, man? I mean, you usually don't drop in. Somebody fuckin' with you at work?"

"Nah, nothing like that. I wish it were something less complicated like that. Remember the barbecue we had at my apartment?"

"Yeah. I had a good time and had been meaning to thank you for the invite. You threw down with the cue too! This got something to do with your friend?"

"Yeah."

Samir leaned over and whispered, "That's a fine ass woman, Max." His remarks were cut short by Yvette as she walked out of the kitchen carrying two Bud longnecks in her hands. Yvette still had her work clothes on, but was sporting her slippers.

"Hey, Max! How you doing, baby? Samir . . . be sure to use them coasters on my table."

Yvette turned around and headed back to her kitchen.

Samir made sure Yvette was out of earshot before he resumed with, "She not pregnant, huh?"

"Oh no, man! It's not like that. I need some advice. You see. I'm crazy about her. But there's a problem."

"She got a man."

"Yep. How'd you know?"

"Lucky guess. Man, you get used to that out here. Goes with the turf. That's why finding that special someone is all the more important. You think she's that 'someone'?"

"Yep. I still have some doubts though. Her man paid me a visit. She's engaged y'know."

"What?! Oh shit. That's not good, man. Any drama?"

"Nothing major. I cleaned up most of the mess already."

Samir squinted as he examined my face more closely and said, "Uh huh. Your nose is still swollen a little. Max, you got a bright future. I don't want to hear about you on the news. Promise me that."

"I promise."

"Boy, boy, boy. That's not cool. Have you guys . . . ?"

"No. We didn't."

"You love her, Max?"

" . . . I don't know. I don't want to consider that right now."

"I can tell she cares for you, but you need to be real with her. She needs to do the same, son. Somebody's gonna wind up getting hurt more than they have been if you don't do that."

"You seem so happy with your family, Samir. I hope I can have half of what you've got one day."

"You'll get yours, Max. When it's right, you'll know . . . and nothing will be able to stop you."

35 *Glover*

Lionel was right about my having to make choices. My little squawk session with Mona helped solidify my decision. Max and I needed to air everything out and leave it behind us. Part of me was still fighting my decision. I decided to compromise between my two conflicting sides and go out with Max one last time. It would be kind of a farewell to our situation. I called Max from my job that Friday. When he answered the phone, he seemed a little distant. I asked him out once I made sure his schedule was clear for the night. He paused then agreed to it. We agreed on House of Blues down on Sunset. Max hadn't been there and I would finally get to see him in a different environment.

I sped home from work and jumped out of my work clothes. I reached in the back of my closet and pulled out my spaghetti-strapped red dress. It was still in the dry cleaner's bag. My t-strap red sandals were sitting in the middle of my shoe rack when I picked them up and dusted them off. I took a quick glance at my layered bob in the mirror on my way to the shower. I didn't need it all droopy tonight and slipped my shower cap on.

I showed up at Max's door looking all sassy and elegant as usual. He was ready when I arrived and hurried out the door. I thought it was a little strange. It was as if he didn't want me to see the place, but maybe he didn't trust the two of us alone in his apartment anymore. I blew the matter off as we headed to House of Blues. Max was wearing a black, long sleeved shirt with olive slacks. His cologne smelled good as usual. I noticed the little hoop earring hanging from his left lobe. This was my first time seeing him with an earring, but the look was working with his athletic build. I had to hand it to him; Max was looking positively delicious. Down, girl. It was going to make it harder to have our little talk later in the night. The drive was mostly silent. We were on North La Cienega heading toward Sunset in my little Civic. Captains was on the right and it had its usual long line in front. Max's attention shifted to it as we passed and his gaze lingered.

"Would you prefer to go to Captains, Max? We can if you want."

"No. No. I was just thinking about something. I've been there before anyway."

"Did you see any stars?"

"Heh. No. Just Smitty and my cousin, *the football player*."

"Your cousin plays ball?"

"No. No. I was joking. Long story."

When we arrived at House of Blues, I embarrassed Max by running around and opening his door for him. We were seated shortly inside the restaurant section. After appetizers, I proposed ordering for each other. Max had started loosening up again. That warm smile had returned to his face; that smile that I loved so much. Max ordered my entrée, the crawfish and shrimp etouffee with white rice. Max told me to go light with his. It was Latin music night in the club section and Max didn't want anything weighing him down. I ordered the roasted salmon for him. I would finally get to check out Max's moves on the dance floor. We women always watch a brother's moves on the floor for obvious reasons. I never got to the obvious reason with Max and that would be a moot point after tonight anyway.

After we finished our meal, we sat around and engaged in small talk. We both seemed to be holding stuff back for later. Was he thinking the same thing? After a few drinks, the check, and tip, we were ready to hit the club.

I listened to Latin music sparingly, but that didn't stop me from dancing my ass off. I did recognize Elvis Crespo and DLG as well as some Spanish language versions of top 40 hits. Meringue and Salsa played most of the night as well as some of that Miami booty shakin' stuff. Max truly surprised me that night. He seemed more comfortable than me on the dance floor. We held hands from time to time as we danced, but I tried to keep the grinding to a minimum. It was hard to do in this atmosphere. Some of the Hispanic patrons looked on and smiled approvingly as Max gyrated like a madman. I was looking on with approval as well, but for different reasons. We burned a lot of calories that night while out on the floor.

While we danced, I said, "I'm impressed. I didn't know you had it in you."

"What?"

"Your dancing, Max. You are *good*."

"*Muchas gracias, Señora* McDaniel. I'll come clean. I've never been to this House of Blues before tonight, but I've been to the one in New Orleans twice. I love to dance. I just don't get much of a chance since moving here."

I smiled and said, "And here I thought you were just a slow country boy."

"Glover, are you going to talk or dance?"

We left for Max's apartment around two o'clock in the morning. I was worn out, so Max drove my car. The mood was still upbeat until we walked into Max's apartment. The laughter ended as Max remembered why he kept me out earlier. Max's living room looked different. Things were missing or rearranged. Two pictures were still in their frames, but the glass was missing and they were on the floor propped against the wall. Max's coffee table was missing also. Max could tell that I noticed the difference and his whole demeanor changed.

"Max, what happened in here?"

"Why don't you ask Lionel, your fiancé? He can fill you in."

I shouted, "So you weren't going to tell me about this?"

"Nope. It was no big deal. We just had a difference of opinion. I can't blame him though. You *are* his woman, right?"

"His 'woman'? You make it sound like I'm someone's property and shit."

"You know what I mean, Glover. Shit! You're about to be married, woman! We're carrying on like we're just friends, but we both know it's more than that, girl! A *lot* more."

"Yeah. We need to talk. Now. I'm glad you reminded me."

Max said with a sorrowful look on his face, "You're right about that. I was going to bring it up earlier, but we were having such a good time . . . "

"So, it's come to this."

"Yep. Glover . . . I want you. I want you more than anything in the world . . . but not like this. This needs to be resolved . . . one way or the other."

"I had such a great time tonight. I really didn't want it to end. I . . . we can't see each other anymore, Max. I'm sorry."

"Don't be. Things are back to the way they should be." Max wouldn't look at me.

"Max . . . I . . ."

"I think you better leave, Glover. Now." Max rested his head on the wall. His eyes were closed tightly and his fists were clenched. To try to stay right now would be sabotaging everything. Max deserved better.

I cried as I drove home. My mascara ran down my face and its nasty taste was on my lips. That night, I would cry myself to sleep and would wake up to a whole new day. The time since I first met Max had been very short, but that time was one of the sweetest times of my life.

36 *Max*

It was tearing my heart out to talk to Glover like that and to let her walk out. It had to be this way. I moved toward the door, but stopped as it closed. I slumped to the floor with my back against the door. I closed my eyes and banged the back of my head against the door out of frustration.

After sitting there in silence, I picked myself up and went to my bedroom. I collapsed across my bed with my sweaty clothes on. I tried to fall asleep, but wound up tossing and turning. It was pointless. I gave up on the sleep option after half an hour. I walked into the kitchen while scratching my head. I decided to drown my sorrows until I fell asleep. The refrigerator light reflected off the six-pack of beer as if it were a sign. I carried the six-pack over to the couch. I normally would have placed the beer on my coffee table, but that was gone now. I pulled one can free and left the rest on the floor on the side of the couch. As I opened the can, I noticed a small rip on the armrest; a reminder of my "disagreement" with Lionel no doubt. I let out a weak laugh as I pushed the "on" button on the TV remote.

I sat on the couch flipping channels between ESPN and Nick at Nite while finishing off the six-pack. I had a good buzz going, but it didn't kill the hurt and confusion I was feeling. Maybe it was my buzz, maybe I knew what I was doing, but it was almost four o'clock in the morning as I walked over to my phone. I opened the drawer on the night stand and looked inside. In the back corner behind the West-tel phone book, were two discarded pieces of paper. I opened the yellow piece first. Scribbled on it was the girl from Captains, Diane's, number. I took a deep breath as I stared down at her number. She had really floated my boat that night, but the thought of her doing anything with Brandi and Jay left a knot in my stomach. There were too many lies wrapped around that night anyway. On the white notepad paper was Valerie's number. I honestly never planned on calling her, especially after meeting Glover, but I convinced my semi-drunk ass that she might be willing to take my mind off things. To hell with the time.

I walked back to the couch and took a seat. I hit the "mute" button on the TV. The phone rang twice when I began to hang up. I had realized that what I was doing was pretty childish and senseless when the phone was answered.

"Hello?" It was a man's voice. A groggy man that I had disturbed. I wasn't positive about the voice, but I think it belonged to another brother. It would have been stupid to think I was the only one or even her first.

"Sorry. Wrong number."

"Awight, dude. *Click*."

I hung up the phone and carried my pitiful ass to bed.

Four hours later, the small slits of sunlight coming through my blinds brought me out of my coma. My breath reeked of beer, my throat was dry and I had a pounding headache to boot. I had never felt more alone in L.A. I needed to get away and clear my head.

I paged Jay and waited. It didn't take long before my phone rang.

"Hello?"

"Country, that you?"

"Cut that shit out."

"Alright. Whaddup?"

"I need a favor. Can you still get me a hook-up on plane flights?"

"Yeah, cuz. I just need to make some calls. Gotta be sure she ain't went and got fired on me n' shit. When you need this?"

"For today if she can. I want go back home for the week-end."

"F' real? Oh shit. If I hook you up, you better bring me back some boudin."

Jay had a "lady friend" that worked at a travel agency in Santa Monica. He had told me about her a while back and how she could get discount tickets. Jay always had someone around town to get the hook-up from and loved to brag about it. Jay's bragging wasn't in vain this time.

Two hours later I was sitting in Jay's Bimmer and still nursing a headache. My duffel bag was in the trunk and we were on our way to Terminal One at LAX. Jay had told me the ticket would be waiting at the airline counter. I called Samir earlier to let him know I was going out of town for a few days. Samir had laughed and said, "That girl got you running of town." I didn't reply. Samir was right.

"You know you coulda' let me know about this earlier. I haven't been to Lake Charles since that last funeral. Coulda' freaked me some big, fine country girls. Shit. I gotta work though."

"Sorry, cuz. I didn't know I was going 'til today. Anyway, Lake Charles isn't *that* country. Shit. You make it sound like people are walking around barefoot with tumbleweeds in their mouths."

"Whatever. I ain't worrying about no tumbleweeds. Bitches out there can walk around barefoot with my dick in their mouth though. Haha."

"Okay. How much do I pay at the counter?"

"Don't worry about that, cuz. I took care of ya. Just don't forget to bring back that boudin. That's some good shit. I wish I could find some out here."

"Alright, Jay. I owe you, cuz."

"You know Pops gonna want you to come by for dinner when you get back. I'm sure he's gonna quiz you about what's going on in Lake Charles."

I don't know what Jay had to do or say, but I didn't pay anything for the ticket. I caught up on my sleep during the flight from LAX to Houston. I had a short layover in H-town before taking a smaller plane on the connecting flight to Lake Charles.

I didn't call my mom, Orelia, as I wanted to surprise her. I took a cab to my mom's house from the airport. I had been gone less than a year, but there were already new restaurants and car dealerships along Highway 14. The area was still changing due to the gambling riverboats that had been here for the past six years. The gambling brought an influx of money into the economy from nearby Texas. With the money came the business boom, but also the loss of innocence that Lake Charles used to have. Things seemed a lot faster in Lake Charles after that as well as more dangerous.

The taxicab turned off Highway 14 and onto Oak Park Boulevard where my mom's house was. We had moved across Highway 14 to Oak Park from the Terrace when my father died years ago. The Terrace was a predominantly black neighborhood populated by a lot of Creoles, a large number of which worked across the lake in the chemical plants, including my dad. My mom couldn't bear the memories when he died in the explosion, so we left our house on Admiral Nimitz and she had been in her brick home in Oak Park ever since. Oak Park was predominantly white at that time, but time seems to change all.

I saw the blinds move when the cab pulled up in the driveway behind her Camry. Orelia always kept an eye open for strange cars in the neighborhood. I was paying the cabby when my mom ran out.

My mom squealed, "Oh, my baby!" and almost picked me up with her hug. I gave her a loving kiss on the cheek and returned the hug. A mother's love was something special.
It felt good to see my mom, but I felt a little out of place being back in Louisiana. The area was still changing, but so was I. It was like taking a fish out of the fish bowl, throwing him into an Olympic-size pool, and then putting him back in the bowl. My mom was disappointed when she saw only my duffel bag and she was even more upset to find out I was only in town until Monday.

"Baby, you sure you don't want to come home to stay?"

"I'm sure, mom. I just needed a little break."

"You don't have somebody pregnant out there, huh?" What was this? Was my mom hanging out with Samir?

"Mom, you know better. Can't I just come down to visit?"

"Yeah, but you didn't sound like you had any plans last time I talked to you. You hungry?"

"No, mom. Just tired."

"Go on back there and get some sleep then. We'll visit when you get up, baby."

I headed back to my old room with my duffel bag dragging behind me. On the hallway walls were framed pictures of our family. I snarled at my kindergarten picture as I walked by. God, I hated that picture. I had a big bush on my head and a tooth missing in the front.

As I disappeared into the back, my mom inquired, "Maxwell, are you going to see that Pitre girl while you here? I saw her in Prien Lake Mall a few weeks back. She said to tell you 'Hi.'"

Denessa Pitre and I were an item for many years, but we broke up and she wound up getting pregnant for one of my boys three months later. I never filled my mom in on the details. I hadn't really thought about Denessa until now, but she still held a special spot in my heart. It was over, but cordial.

I threw my bag on the floor and kicked my shoes off. I was about to snooze, but decided to get the phone first. I called my number in L.A. to see if any messages were left. None.

"Stupid, man. Stupid," I thought to myself as I walked back to my old room.

37
Glover

The wild ride I had been on had come to an end. The dangerous game was over for me. I did not pass "GO", I didn't collect $200, but on the other hand I didn't go straight to jail either. But enough with the metaphors. The choice was made. I would be Mrs. Lionel Dunning and everything would be fine.

I cried myself to sleep after leaving Max's apartment and woke up looking like shit on a very short stick. I showered, got myself right, and called my girls Saturday morning. I had an afternoon appointment scheduled for me at the bridal studio on Wilshire. Last minute fitting adjustments were needed for my bridal gown. Mona and Charmaine needed to be fitted also. Mona was my matron of honor and Charmaine was my main bridesmaid. Lionel's sister, Sarabeth, who was flying in from Europe and his first cousin, Jazelle, were the other bridesmaids.

I surprised myself when I called Lionel to ask if he wanted to tag along. Lionel was even more surprised, but agreed. I left the apartment and stopped at the post office to put invitations in the mail. I picked up Mona and Charmaine on the drive-by and met up with Lionel in Beverly Hills in front of the studio. Lionel was standing outside the studio exuding his usual confidence. He was wearing one of his white linen shirts and a pair of black denims.

The whole studio was ours during our appointment. Lionel's mother had scheduled it as she had been scheduling everything in preparation for the event. I had gone through the motions before, but I was determined to play a more active role from now on. I still was uncomfortable with the pampering and money being spent, but Charmaine and Mona had no problems. This middle-aged white man named Carlo greeted us at the door. He was wearing all black, was thin and feminine-like in his mannerisms and wore his black hair in a short ponytail. Carlo hemmed and hawed around me while his fellow handlers served complimentary champagne to Mona and Charmaine. Lionel just sat back and watched with amusement. My gown was being finalized and samples were sitting on a small mahogany end table next to the highback chair Charmaine was in.

"G-love, you sure about the dress?" Charmaine asked as she held a sample in one hand and an empty champagne glass in the other. "What about Nicole Miller or Escada?"

"Charmaine. Shush," I said as I gave her a disapproving glance. Their dresses were nice too, but I wasn't going to say it out loud. I noticed that my seamstress/tailor had heard Charmaine's remarks too. Carlo stood motionless with one eyebrow raised before he resumed fussing over me. The last thing I needed was getting him ticked off and sticking me with a needle.

"I think Charmaine's enjoying the freebies a little too much," Mona said as she walked around the studio.

"Girl, you don't know what you're talking about. I've only had two of these little glasses for your information. You need to loosen up yourself." Charmaine then stuck her tongue out at Mona.

Lionel was having a blast watching this and tried not to snicker. I could only imagine what the wedding would be like with these two in it. I suggested that the other handlers start measuring Mona and Charmaine to keep them out of each other's hair. Now it was time for Mona's size eight and Charmaine's size twelve frame to be wrapped, taped, and measured like fashion mummies.

As I excused myself to go to the restroom, I asked Mona if I could borrow her cell phone. She pointed to her purse, which was resting near the walkway. I walked right past her purse on the way to the restroom and casually lifted her phone out. I had to call Max to make sure he was okay. Even though our "relationship" was over, I still cared about his well being. It would be very cold not to check up on him.

I opened the restroom door and walked in. I sat down in one of the upholstered chairs just inside and dialed. The phone rang several times and I hung up just as the answering machine clicked on. No need letting my thoughts wander and rambling on tape. I could wind up saying something inappropriate and mess up Max's life again. He was too good a man for that.

I stayed in the restroom for a minute longer and splashed some water on my face. I was beginning to run on empty. The night before with Max and the lack of sleep was wearing on me. A little food in my tummy would provide a quick fix.

When I walked back to the front of the studio, Carlo had moved on to Mona and Charmaine. His fellow handlers were scurrying about as he barked out orders to them. I slipped Mona's cell phone back into her purse and continued my walk toward them. I slowed by Mona.

Mona cracked a smile and whispered, "Had to call him, huh?"

"Shhhhh," I responded. "It's all over. I was just checking on him. For real."

"If you say so, *Mrs. Dunning*."

"*Oh*. You say it so elegantly, Mona," I laughed.

"Would a diva do it any other way?" Mona replied as she struck a pose with measuring tape dangling off her waist. It was a *very* funny sight to behold. I think the free champagne had loosened her up too.

"We need to get Charmaine some food, Glover. Her ass is tipsy and about to fall over."

"Sounds good to me. Pizza anyone?"

38

Max

I didn't miss the heat and humidity in Louisiana. It was only springtime, but it felt like I was walking around under somebody's armpit. Almost ninety degrees. Lucky for me I was leaving for L.A. tomorrow. I had spent the previous night catching up with my mom and visiting relatives once I woke up and shook the jet lag off. I sat in the kitchen that night and chowed down on a bowl of okra and rice, just like old times. I promised my mom that I would wash her car first thing this morning. Since my Celica was thousands of miles away, Orelia was going to let me roll in her Camry after cleaning it. It would be a windows-up kind of day with this kind of heat.

The car wash on Highway 14 was only a few blocks away. When I was in high school, it used to be the spot to show off your ride or at least your rims if you were pushing a hooptie like Smitty's. The cops used to run us off at night when the crowds would get too "uncomfortable" for them to put up with. It was just a normal self-service car wash with stalls and vacuum cleaners, but in a town with not a whole lot to do it was the place to be. Times changed and the violence picked up. Young brothers thinking they had something to prove and the dope game brought a whole different atmosphere. A town that was already eager to control its minority population was quick to jump in. The light faded. The place was back to being simply a car wash now.

I had my mom's ride covered in suds when an old blue Caddy rolled by slowly. The car was older than I was, but the little baby gangsters inside were younger. The passenger had a mouth full of gold teeth, but I couldn't tell with the driver. We exchanged nods as their car rolled past my stall while I resumed scrubbing. I guess they were wondering who the "old nigger" was. Heh.

Twenty minutes later I was rolling down 14 in my mom's clean car. I missed getting a quick haircut so I continued North until Highway 14 turned into MLK. I was passing Fisherville and heading into Goosport. I made a left turn onto Opelousas Street to go to Mr. Thomas' barbershop for a fresh cut. Mr. Thomas was there in his barbershop across the street from Immaculate Heart Church as sure as clockwork. I was the only customer so I jumped straight in the barber chair. While I got an edge and trim, I filled him in on how things were going with me in California. Mr. Thomas said that he would say a few prayers for me on the job front and told me to just believe. He followed it up with a smile and wink that seemed to indicate he was in on something special. I gave him an extra tip and patted him on the back before leaving out the door and down the steps. When I was backing out into the street I thought about Mr. Thomas' words when I walked in.

"I've been waiting for you," he said. I blew it off until just then when I realized what day it was. Mr. Thomas' barbershop was always closed on Sunday and Monday. A chill ran down my spine until I shook it off and drove away.

I guess it was idle curiosity that made me pay a visit to Denessa next. I heard she was still staying at her apartment on Fifth Avenue across town. The place was more run down than I remembered. Maybe my short time away had made me more critical. A brand new complex was springing up next door. I wondered if it would be the next one to become neglected. Denessa stayed in building J, apartment 104. It was years in the past now, but I remembered the wild times we had in there, especially during finals. Down boy. That ended under less than great terms then she gets knocked up by a friend. Even with that drama, we were cool whenever we ran into each other. The past was in the past, both here and in L.A.

I didn't see Denessa's car on the parking lot. She may have been working, but I was just stopping in to say 'Hi' anyway. There was a piece of folded paper jammed in between the door-knob and the frame. I didn't hear any noise coming from inside as I knocked on the door. Nothing. I gave one more courtesy knock and waited.

"You a relative?" I heard come from the next doorway over.

"No. I was just passing by," I said as I backed up and looked in the direction of the other apartment.

"Max? That's you?" The figure came out of the doorway. A round droopy-eyed brother was wiping the cold from his eyes as he stepped into the light. My memory was jogged.

"Cujo?" Yep, it was him. Cujo or Troy, his real name, went to high school with me back at LaGrange. He was an all-star lineman who went to LSU on scholarship. He was definitely a first round draft pick until he screwed up his knee. He was drunk one night on campus and tried to jump out a second story win-dow. End of career.

"Hey, Max. What's up, dawg? You still livin' out here?"

"Nah, dawg. Moved to Cali."

"Oh. That's tight. You musta heard about Denessa."

"No. What's up?"

"It was all over the news. She gone, man. Her, her little girl, and this dude from Houston. They was movin' to Houston with cuz and he fell asleep behind the wheel and shit. Happened on I-10 just past Beaumont. Damn shame. Hey . . . you two used to date, huh?"

"Yeah."

I went back to my mother's house and stayed there until it was time to leave. Orelia was stunned when I told her about what happened to Denessa. She then called her town grapevine and confirmed it. The Internet had nothing on the grapevine. I gave my mom some money to put in on some flowers for Denessa's family. She was going to pick them up the next day to deliver them. There was a sad silence in the car as Orelia brought me to the airport Monday. She knew I had shit on my mind. Her last words were spoken halfway to herself and halfway to me.

"I thought the two of you would get back together one day," she sighed as we drove down Common Street. I didn't respond.

It wasn't until I made it back inside my apartment that I remembered. Jay wanted some boudin. I was gonna hear it from him, but he would just have to find some out here. It was after midnight and the TV was watching me as I darted back and forth putting things up. I didn't have to be at Denny's until Tuesday evening so I would have time to crash. I just had restless energy as I was trying to go over all the recent events in my head. I was too young for this. I turned off the TV and put on my old Keith Sweat CD instead. I put the player on "random" after I selected the CD. My stereo wasn't even close to Smitty's houseshaker, but I turned it up anyway. I then jumped into the shower and left the door open so I could sing along.

"Toss and turn and yearning . . . I just can't sleep at night . . . Ooo. You've been cheatin' on me. Tell me, it's a lie . . ."

39   *Glover*

Monday was typically busy. The wedding preparation had kicked into high gear and my bridal jitters were starting to flare up. Mona and Charmaine, the true friends that they are, made fun of me every chance they got. They were looking forward to the wedding and reception at Catalina. Money was going to be in the air that day and landing an available, financially stable brother would be on their minds. I had mailed invitations to my people back in Virginia, but I doubted they would show up, especially with the short notice. I didn't keep up with them once my grandmother passed away. When my mom died, a few cousins came down for the funeral, but that was it. I never really knew my dad's people and I had no idea if he was even alive. Lionel's dad had volunteered to walk me down the aisle and I was probably going to take him up on that offer. Maybe that was another reason I didn't want a church wedding. It just didn't feel right with this situation. I mean with my mom gone. The last time I had stepped foot in a church was for my mother's funeral; the day my best friend was gone for good. It was an issue with me and I still hadn't dealt with it.

I considered spending the night at Lionel's after work, but after stopping off at the apartment to change. I had resisted this long, but maybe it was time to start moving a few things over there. I had an unpleasant surprise when I jumped on I-10 after work. Some idiot in a stolen car had wiped out after a police chase and most of the westbound lanes had to be closed down.

It wasn't until after eight o'clock that night that I came dragging in through my front door. I dropped my purse on the floor, kicked my shoes off my feet, dove onto my sofa. I was too exhausted to even eat and arched back as I slipped my bra off and undid the button on my skirt. I let out a sigh of relief as my slip had been rubbing my waist raw all day. The red skirt looked good on me, but it was getting a little snug and would have to go. Mona was smaller. Maybe she would have use for it. I leaned back again as I slid my pantyhose down and pulled them off. The slip followed. My dogs had been sore since the weekend. I did a lot of walking and standing Saturday during the fitting and stuff, but most of the pain was from Friday night. I smiled as I rubbed the arches of my feet. My thoughts drifted to Max and of my trying to keep up with him on the dance floor. It was a nice feeling of freedom out there with just the music and the two of us.

I chuckled before pulling myself up from the sofa. I poured myself a glass of white wine before sitting back down and drifting asleep. My last coherent thought was that I was to spend the night at Lionel's. A quick nap before going there wouldn't hurt.

As I slept, I dreamed I was flying high above the clouds. I was naked and soaring over green mountains with waterfalls everywhere. I felt the wind on my face and all across my body as I started doing loopty-loops through the clouds. I never had a dream like this. This was fun. As soon as I got used to the flying experience, the weather suddenly changed. The white, fluffy clouds turned dark and stormy. Lightning was flashing everywhere and the thunder was deafening. Rain started hammering me to the point where I couldn't see. I was suddenly falling from the sky. I plunged through the clouds and the ground was getting closer and closer. I started screaming and flailing around in vain. My heart felt like it wanted to burst through my chest. I tried to close my eyes, but couldn't. Just when I had given up all hope, I landed in the arms of . . . ."

I sat up in a panic on my sofa. I was still in my shirt and skirt from work. I looked toward my blinds. Outside I could hear the rain crashing against the window. I was looking at the "12:15" that was displayed on my clock when the thunder roared and sent a flash of lightning across my apartment. I had slept that long? I had only meant to take a short nap before going to Lionel's. I knew I couldn't stay here though. Thunderstorms still spooked me and my dream still had me rattled. I put my shoes back on, grabbed my purse, and ran out the door of my apartment. I hadn't realized how hard the rain was coming down until I was outside running in it. My umbrella was in the car. I was drenched, but the awning over my parking spot gave me a break while I fumbled for my keys. Lionel was probably asleep, so I would just have to wake him up.

I drove my Civic west down San Vicente until I came to Hauser Boulevard. The light was red and the rain had actually picked up. I focused on the wiper blades as they went back and forth. They were having trouble keeping up with the downpour, so I sped them up with a twist of the handle. I was behind an old truck while waiting for the light to turn green. All I had to do was make a right turn to head to Lionel's. A left turn would take me down Hauser to Venice Boulevard where Max lived. Lightning danced and lit up the sky. It must have struck nearby because the thunder boomed right after. The light turned green. Time to make that right turn. And I drove off.

When I arrived, I thought about running to the back of the car to fish out my umbrella. The rain wasn't coming down as hard, but it was still consistent. I decided to run for it instead. I almost slipped in a puddle and bust my ass on the way to the door. As I approached the door, I could hear music playing. Heh. I knew the song too. Wasn't expecting to hear music at this time of night. I thought that maybe company was being entertained and almost didn't knock. When I knocked I heard the music lower, then footsteps. I must have been a pretty sick sight when the door opened. The song that was playing was "Right and A Wrong Way". Max was standing there wearing nothing, but a blue towel. He paused when he saw me. I was still dripping in his hallway.

"Ar . . . are you okay?" he asked while looking at me.

"Yeah. Just a little wet. Heh. I hate thunderstorms. You have company?"

"No, no company."

"You smell good."

"Yeah. It's called soap. Look . . . Glover, I don't have time for this. You have to leave."

I walked into his apartment and pushed the door shut behind me. I was right up against his chest when I put my fingers to his lips and whispered, "Shhhh. Don't say a thing. I need you. *Now.*"

I stepped out of my wet shoes and stood on one leg while I pulled Max down into me. My other bare leg rubbed up against his. Max began kissing my fingertips that were on his lips, then froze up and tried to back away. His towel had begun to rise up.

He paused, closed his eyes, and then asked, "Are you using me, Glover?"

"Maybe. I don't know."

Max then took a deep breath. That was just before he lunged back toward me. His kisses on my neck where setting me on fire. My head flew back as I sucked on my bottom lip in delight.

In the middle of his kisses, Max whispered in my ear, "What are you doing here?"

40

Max

"I'm here because I want you. I need you," Glover answered. My lips had found their way up to her ear. Normally I would have stopped this on the spot, but things were different tonight. My trip to Lake Charles had me thinking. I learned from what happened to Denessa to live everyday as if it were your last. Glover also caught me in the middle of the night when my resistance was at a low point and while I was just out of the shower with just a towel on. I could have made excuses about the jet lag and everything else, but they wouldn't hold up. I knew what I was doing and so did she.

Our lips found each other and we continued from where we left off on my couch almost a month ago. We stood there kissing as Glover's fingernails ran playfully up and down my back. Glover moaned as I sucked on her tongue. Her hands had worked their way down to my towel and were beginning to tug on it. We walked together while embracing and I backed us up into the bedroom. The song playing on my CD changer was adding to the moment. I snickered inside my head and wondered if the mood would be different if I had my 69 Boys album playing instead.

My towel had come off just before we made it to the bed. Glover had taken me in her left hand and was rubbing it up against her skirt. We backed up into my bed frame when I ran my hands down the small of her lovely back. I then brought my

145

hands down further. I squeezed her ass, as I had wanted to do since I first saw the bubble and then went down to the back of her thighs. I almost immediately went up under her skirt as we continued kissing. Glover let out a half-moan/half-whisper as I gripped her bare ass cheeks with both hands. Glover had nothing on underneath the red skirt. I brought my right hand up and yanked on the button on the side of the skirt. The button went flying and the zipper gave way simultaneously. The skirt fell to the bedroom floor and came to rest on her feet. Glover then stepped out of the heap of fabric.

Glover looked at me and laughed, "I was going to get rid of that skirt anyway."

She then started kissing me on my chest and ran her lips across my nipples before pushing me down onto my bed.

I was caught off guard and landed on a stack of my clothes that I hadn't put up yet since returning from my trip. It didn't matter as I swatted them onto the floor.

Glover stood there over me at the foot of my bed. I was on my back with my hard-on saluting her. Glover was still wet, but was looking like she just stepped out of some photo shoot waterfall. All that remained on her was her damp, white blouse. Her bare breasts were visible through the wet fabric. The light from my bathroom was reflecting off her face revealing those crazy, sexy eyes of hers. She was smiling wickedly as she started slowly unbuttoning her top. The shirt was just long enough to cover her lower area and to make her striptease all the more enticing. When Glover was down to the last two buttons, I stood back up and whipped Glover around to where her back was facing me. I stood right up against her where she could feel me pushing between her legs from behind. It seemed almost like she wanted to rest on it and take the load off her feet. It was rigid all right, just not a 2 X 4. I reached around and brought my hands down her front and between her erect breasts. I helped Glover with the last two buttons and she straightened her arms to let her shirt fall off.

I then left Glover standing there as I sat down at the foot of the bed. I gripped her waist while she called my name slowly at first. As I ran my tongue slowly up her back, her chanting became more rapid and louder. I tasted the distinctive, salty flavor of sweat mixed faintly with rainwater. This was Glover's sweat and it turned me on even more.

I brought my tongue up to her neck and started flicking my tongue into her ear. Glover reached back with both hands and brought them to rest behind my head as she ran her fingers through my hair. Just then there was a loud burst of thunder outside followed by the rain picking up. The heat in the room was working up to a fever pitch.

I brought my hands to rest on the underside of Glover's golden breasts then slowed worked my fingers up around her areolas. Glover dropped her hands in response and had reached around to my hips. I noticed that we were in front of my mirror as this was going on. Glover was looking into the mirror as well and I saw her smile and wink at me. Glover began to back into me and started pulling me harder into her as my fingers ran across her nipples and started making little circles across the tops of them. We both watched this in front of the mirror. It was kinda freaky, but kinda cool at the same time.

Glover had reached her limit and I was pretty close too as she turned around to face me. She then took my hands in hers and slowly lowered herself down onto the bed. I straddled on top of her as I kissed her inner thighs then belly button. She then pulled me onto her and begged me to enter. I was more than willing to oblige and Glover let out an "Oh!" as I began to penetrate her. Glover arched her beautiful body in a spasm of delight as I went deeper. Glover's legs began to wrap around behind me as she urged me on further. Her wetness made it easier for me to continue on. The storm outside was nothing compared to the one raging inside the walls of my bedroom. Glover and I continued on until drenched with sweat. She climaxed several times as her trembling and moaning would announce each one's arrival. When I was about to come my first time, she reached down to slow me and gave me a look that told me she was in control. Her hands reached down and squeezed my scrotum until the moment had subsided. She may have been making a mistake this night, but was going to get everything out of it. We eventually wound up climaxing simultaneously as my toes curled up and I fell to her side. Glover let out a low whimper, as she lay there covered in sweat with her eyes tightly closed. She had the nail of her pinkie finger clenched between her teeth and had begun laughing with delight.

Once I was coherent, I turned over on my side and looked at Glover. The words just rolled from my mouth. I was still living in the moment and to hell with the consequences.

"Glover, I think I might be falling in love with you." It was a word I had intentionally avoided.

She smiled at me and replied "Don't say that, Max." and left me in the bed to get some bottled water from my kitchen.

I caught my breath in the bed while Glover was in my fridge. She returned with the opened bottle of water in her hand. This was my first time to really take everything in. There was so much happiness in her smile at this point. I had gotten to know so much about Glover over the last month and a half, but tonight had brought me even further emotionally and physically. We held back nothing and I had bared my soul this night. Time would tell if Glover would bare hers or if she even knew what was really there.

"Are you okay?" she playfully asked while climbing back into the bed.

"Fine. Couldn't be better. Don't worry about what I said earlier. I just had to get that out. I'm not gonna be trippin'." Glover reached out and handed the water to me.

"Okay. You know what?"

"What?" I asked as I guzzled down the rest of the water.

"This was *incredible*. I mean it."

"Thanks, I guess."

"But . . . "

"But what?"

"It's not over."

Glover then reached down between my legs and started stroking me with her hand. I could feel the blood rushing back there again.

41

Glover

"I feel like I need a cigarette," Max said as we cuddled in his bed and looked into each other's eyes. It was four o'clock and I had to be to work in four hours.

I laughed, "Those things are bad for you, Max."

"I'm just kidding. What are you doing here anyway?"

"I thought it was obvious, " I said as I smiled and gestured at our naked bodies.

"Cute. You know what I mean."

"I had a crazy dream and you were in it. I woke and was spooked. I just knew that I needed to see you. I didn't like the note things ended on last time."

"Oh. I see your ring is missing again. Forgot it?"

"No, not this time. I left it in my car when I was certain about what I was doing. I almost didn't come here. I was trying to fight it with all my heart."

"I guess your heart gave up. You never really told me much about him. What does he do?"

"He works downtown at B&G."

"Barnes & Greenwood? I thought he looked familiar . . . when we 'met'. I had been in the Gas Company Tower the day I met you. Maybe I saw him downtown somewhere."

"Maybe. You two got in a fight, huh? Shit. I *knew* it. I am just so stupid," I said as I slapped my forehead and sat up in the bed. I pulled the sheet up to my chest. "Max, I am sorry. Really. This is all my fault."

Max slid over to me and wrapped his warm arms around me. "Shhh. What's done is done. I'm as much to blame in this as anyone."

" I saw your clothes on the bed. Were you going somewhere tonight?"

"Nah. Actually, I was just getting back. I went home for a few days."

"Oh. It was hard on you too. I'm sorry."

"Sheesh. Enough with the apologies already, " Max said as he tickled me. I felt such electricity when I was with him.

"You know my wedding is coming up soon."

"Yep. I've been checking my mailbox everyday for the invitation. You think my mailman took it?"

"Har. Har. Something's different about you, Max."

"Yep. A lot has happened since you last saw me. My perspective's a little different now. It's still me though."

"Yeah. That smile is still the same," I said as I turned to kiss him. I pushed Max down onto the bed and climbed on top of him as we continued to kiss. We wound up doing the do again. It was close to dawn and I knew I needed to get home, but part of me didn't want to leave. Once I left outside of this bubble, I was afraid of things going back to the way they were. That's life I guess. The illusion has to give way to reality. We never brought up Max's comment about falling in love with me. It was something I didn't forget though.

Max was kind enough to let me use his shower and even let me borrow a pair of his warm-up bottoms. I could have used a safety pin to hold my skirt up, but some of my older neighbors would have been gossiping. We gave each other a quick kiss as I rushed out the door and to my Civic. My ring was sitting there right by the gearshift where I left it hours ago. I paused then closed my eyes as I placed the ring back on my finger. I rushed home and was pulling into the parking lot as the sun started rising above the clouds. It was going to be another smoggy day. At least the thunderstorms had passed in the night. The damp ground was the only reminder of the stormy night. That, and my sore body. Whew! I finally got to see those shoulders of his in action and the pleasure was all mine.

I made it in to work on time. I was run down, but tried to play it off. I stopped at a Korean mini-mart on the way in and bought one of those vitamin energy packs and a bottle of Gatorade. Mr. Marx had hired some more people and things were at a bearable pace around the office. That was especially welcome on a day like today. The three amigas got to take a break together in the morning for the first time in weeks.

"G-love, are we doing anything this weekend? We've haven't been out clubbing since that time at Drama." Charmaine smiled as she cut a sly look at Mona. Club Drama was still a touchy subject with Mona.

"I wish. I have to go out to Catalina this weekend. The wedding's going to be here before we know it."

Mona asked, "Glover, have you thought about the job here. Are you going to quit?" She was sitting back in one chair with her feet up in another.

"I'm still undecided, Mona. There's so much I haven't had a chance to consider yet."

"You're going to have a bachelorette party, G-love? Cause I know just the strippers to get . . . "

"No! No! None of that! Y'all aren't getting me in trouble!"

"Aww c'mon! You know Lionel's people are gonna throw one for him. Hell, they're probably gonna truck in real live French whores for the event," Charmaine said while she stood up and danced around the break room in a silly manner. We all burst out laughing.

"No, Charmaine. We already talked about that. Lionel's not going to have one either."

" I know I would want to go out with a bang . . . or two," Mona said with a sigh, "but I guess you've made up your mind."

"You guys are right about one thing; the three of us need to do something together before I tie the knot."

"Umm, G-love. I shouldn't bring this up . . . but you are about to be off the market and stuff. I was wondering about that fine ass stud you were talking with in front of the office a while back. Since you don't really have a need for him, I was wondering . . . um . . . if you could hook your friend up. *Oh, the things I could do with him.*"

Mona noticed me blink and flinch in response to Charmaine's last comment and interjected, "Charmaine, please. Glover barely knows that guy. He was just checking on a job that day."

"Oh. Damn, G-love. You shoulda at least got the digits! I guess that's that."

"Sorry, Charmaine." I gave Mona a thank-you look and shrugged my shoulders at Charmaine. Mona was a master at reading people and knew what my flinching meant.
Luckily, our break time was over and we returned to our desks.

I was deep into my work when my phone rang an hour later.

"Ms. McDaniel. May I help you."

"Heh. Heh. I'm calling about an interview." The voice on the other end of the phone perked me up instantly.

"Hey, you," I mumbled with excitement. No need in the office knowing what I was talking about.

"Sorry to bother you, but I had to call. You think you're gonna be hungry Thursday night?"

"Thursday? I guess. Why?"

"No strings or anything. I wanted to know if you wanted some 'dirty south' home cookin'."

"Max, are you cooking for me?"

"Me? No! I'm having dinner at my Uncle Mo's . . . and I'm inviting you as a guest."

42

Max

After Glover left, I went back to the bedroom and lay down. I stared up at the ceiling for about thirty minutes while I reflected on what had just happened. The sun was coming up and the rain had stopped. I needed to get some sleep, but I cleaned up and changed the sheets first. As I slept, I dreamed of making love to Glover over and over again. The damn girl had me feenin' for sure. Being in her company was a powerful drug.

My dreams had ended and given way to the silence of blackness. I was in a deep sleep as my mind and body needed the downtime. It was only the phone ringing that brought me out of it just before noontime.

"Hullo."

"Hey, Country! Yo ass made it back in one piece?"

"Yeah, Jay. Thanks, man. Cuz, I forgot your boudin though."

"Aww. That's fucked up, cuz. Let me guess. You ran into an old girlfriend and she fucked your memory away."

"No. An old girlfriend did die though."

"Yeah, that's really funny. You know you owe me double now."

"Yeah. I know. Can't you get some boudin out here?"

"Hell no, nigga! Don't worry about it. I told Pops you went to Lake Charles. Moms is cookin' Thursday so you know the deal."

"I can make it. Jay, would they mind if I brought some company with me?"

"Not that nigga, Smitty, huh?"

"No. Just a lady friend."

"Oh shit! You got a woman, Country?"

"Naw, man. Just a friend."

Jay tried to get the details out of me, but there was nothing really to tell and I was tired as hell. Besides, I could hear Jay's mouth now if he knew the details. "Country, did you eat some of that girl's red gravy? Cause she got you trippin' and shit." I wasn't sure if Glover would be interested until I called her at work

When I picked up Glover Thursday night, I didn't know what she would be wearing. I played it safe and dressed up a little more than usual for dinner at Uncle Mo's. I wore a dark green button-down with khaki slacks and brown loafers. I was glad I didn't put on warm-ups or something. Glover wore a turquoise knit outfit with flared sleeves and cutout shoulders, which I especially liked. On the drive to Carson, I was tempted to steal a kiss on one of those shoulders, but kept my eyes on the road. I also filled Glover in on the Chavis family before we got there.

The smell of food cooking was in the air as usual when Aunt Verna had a feast, but I should have realized things were different when she answered the door. Aunt Verna was usually in the kitchen when company arrived, but not this time. Jay must have told them that I had company coming over and Aunt Verna wanted to check out Glover first. Aunt Verna even wore makeup on was wearing one of her colorful shirts.

The good plates were out on the table and Uncle Mo, who was already at the table, was wearing one of his nicer golf shirts. Jay had worked late today and was upstairs in his room changing. Dinner included: smothered pork chops with rice and gravy, baked macaroni, green beans, cornbread, and rolls. Glover sat on the side of me and I watched her eyes light up when the food came out. I gave her a playful pinch on the thigh under the table and she grabbed my hand before I could pull it back. She held my hand and gently caressed it with her fingers while Aunt Verna explained the menu and how hard she slaved to cook everything. Uncle Mo had an approving smile as he looked at

Glover then he cut a quick wink at me. I would attempt to explain to him later that we were just friends, but I'm sure he wouldn't believe it. This was the third time Glover left her ring off. I started wishing that maybe it would become a permanent thing-the two of us.

I think I had a secret motive inviting Glover to eat. Uncle Mo and them were the closest family I had out here. I wanted to see Glover through my family's eyes as I was probably less than objective about her right about now. If the remote possibility existed of us somehow getting together, then tonight would give me a good indication about our future.

Uncle Mo looked impatiently toward the stairwell then turned toward us and said, "Glover, you'll have to excuse our boy, Junior, he should be down in a minute."

"That's quite alright, Mr. Chavis. I'm happy to just sit here and enjoy your company."

"Please, call me 'Maurice', girl," Uncle Mo said with a bashful grin. I think his old ass was having a flashback from his days of youth. If he didn't behave, Aunt Verna was probably going to clock him with one of her black cast-iron skillets.

Aunt Verna joined in, "So Glover, do you have any people from Louisiana?"

Glover started laughing and replied, "No, ma'am. Just Virginia." She was probably tired of people asking her the "Louisiana" question.

Just then, Jay came jogging down the stairs. Jay was wearing a red Enyce top with black pants and black Nikes. I stood up to introduce Jay to Glover.

"Whaddup, cuz."

"Whaddup, Jay. This is my friend, Glover. Glover this is my cousin, Jay."

Jay had a strange look on his face as he shook Glover's hand. His eyes were squinty then widened. Glover had her normal smile then suddenly it turned into a scowl. Something was up.

Glover said, "Pleased to meet you . . . "

"Jay. Maurice Jr., but everyone calls me 'Jay'," Jay shot off rapidly and with emphasis.

"Oh. I had you confused with someone else. You ever been to Ohio?" Glover said with a smirk on her face.

"N . . . nah. Just southern Cal," Jay replied before heading to his chair on the side of Uncle Mo.

We sat down to eat after that strange introduction. Over dinner, I noticed Jay's eyes bounce from Glover to me and back again.

I was wiping my mouth after a piece of buttery cornbread when I whispered to Glover, "What's going on?"

"I'll fill you in when we leave," she said while cutting her eyes at Jay.

Both of us were too full for dessert, but took three foil-covered plates with us as we got ready to leave. Aunt Verna was talking it up with Glover as we started heading down the hallway. Jay shot away from the table, but started up the stairs instead. He stopped halfway to where I could only see his legs.

"Ay, cuz. Let me holler at you real quick," came from the half of Jay I could see. I paused to look at Glover. Aunt Verna and Uncle Mo would keep her entertained for a second.

I followed Jay up the stairs and into his room.

"What's up, Jay?"

Jay whipped around like some kind of madman and said, "What the fuck are you doin' with that bitch??!!"

"What are you talking about?"

"That bitch down there! Glover! Man, I thought I knew you better!"

"*Again*, I'm gonna ask you what are you talking about."

"Cuz, I fucked that ho before. I met her at that club, Drama, a while back. Bitch is a real freak. Cuz, I can't believe you're bringing her up in my parents' house," Jay muttered while pointing an accusing finger at me.

"Jay, cut that 'bitch' and 'ho' shit out. You don't know what the fuck you're talking about." I was starting to get a sick, angry feeling in the pit of my stomach.

"Max, I ran into her in the club before. I dropped her a line about being a TV producer and shit. Next I know, 'Bam!' she up in the hotel with me sucking my dick, ass, and whatever else. I know you country and shit, but you can't be that stupid. That bitch playin' you?" I was really feeling sick now.

"You're crazy, man. Fuck you."

"You need to watch your mouth. That bitch got you sprung. If you want to fuck around and be parading around with that ho on your arm, then go ahead. Just don't bring her around here. She nothin' but a freak. How long you known her anyway?"

I ignored Jay's question and started storming out of his room. Answering that question would only help his argument. Jay wouldn't let it end though.

Jay mumbled to himself, "Heh. Bitch was a good fuck though . . . liked to take it from the back."

Bam!

I slugged Jay right in his mouth. Jay fell to the floor with a busted lip. Blood was dripping through his fingers and blending in with his red shirt. I turned back around and headed out the door.

"I warned you about that 'bitch' shit, cuz."

Jay blurted out through his covered mouth, "I hope you get what's coming to you, punk ass nigga! She's gonna probably lie to cover her ass! See if I ever look out for you again!"

Shit. I had scraped one of my knuckles on Jay's teeth.

43 _Glover_

I couldn't believe this shit. Max's cousin was the brother in blue from Club Drama. I think he called himself Cary or Terry that night. I wasn't positive at first, but the way he reacted to me confirmed it. Heh. A really small world. I think he squirmed enough at the dinner table. I just hoped Max was nothing like his fake ass cousin.

While I talked with Max's delightful aunt and uncle, Max had run upstairs. For a second, I thought I heard shouting. Max came down the stairs, said a quick goodbye to his people, then stormed out the door past me. Something was wrong. He was outside on the front lawn before he noticed that I had three plates to carry. Max caught himself and came back to take two of the plates out of my hands. He walked around to my side of the Celica and opened the car door for me. I noticed him flexing his right hand like it was hurt or something.

As we drove up the I-110 ramp to head north to my apartment, I decided to strike up the conversation. Max was being the strong, silent type up to this point.

"Dinner was incredible, Max. Your aunt and uncle were great company. You were too, up until we left."

"Oh. Sorry."

"What's wrong?"

"Nothing."

"Something's wrong. You've clammed up and shit. Is it about your cousin?"

"Yeah. I guess it kinda has to do with him."

"Did he tell you about the club?"

"Yeah. He told me something."

"And?"

"And I punched him out."

"Over that? I mean, he was an asshole, but maybe punching him was a little extreme."

"Naw. I don't think it was too much. So the shit's true then?"

"I guess. I don't like your tone, Max. Wait. Wait. What did he say happened?"

"Some shit about you leaving Drama with him."

"What?! That lying son of a bitch! Max, he tried to pick me up and was dismissed. He was claiming he was a producer or something from Ohio. Even went by a different name."

"Oh."

"Is that all you can say? 'Oh?' Your cousin said something else, huh?"

"Don't worry about it. It's nothing."

"Nothing?! Max, you haven't looked at me since we left. What did he say?"

"I really don't want to talk about it. It's nothing."

"Max . . . did he say he fucked me or something?"

There was silence on his part. I had my answer. Now I was pissed.

I pushed further and asked, "That's what he said, huh? Shit. Ooooh! I *hate* mutherfuckers like that!" Max started to speak then clammed up again.

I swatted at Max out of frustration as I my eyes watered up. "Answer me, dammit! Do you believe him then??!!"

Max blinked then slowly turned. His silent rage was dying down as mine was skyrocketing up. Max let a "No." come slowly out of his lips, but it wasn't adamant.

"Humph. I guess blood is thicker than water. Well, fuck you and your lying ass cousin."

"I said I didn't believe him, Glover."

"It wasn't what you said, but the way you said it."

"How do you expect me to act, Glover? My cousin, who I've known all my life, tells me this bullshit and I wind up clocking him. You, who I've known a couple of months, are on the other side screaming at me because I'm not jumping up and down. C'mon, let's look at our history here . . . " That really hurt. Max had lashed out unintentionally, but it still hurt. Tears were openly streaming down my face now. We were merging onto I-10 west now. I would be home soon.

"I don't blame you, Max. I guess I have been acting like a ho since I met you. Why should you think otherwise or believe me when I say that what's going on with us is the first time I've done something like this."

"Look, Glover . . . I didn't mean it like that. I wasn't trying to hurt you. Jay can be full of shit and I've seen him lie to women in clubs with lines and shit. I'm just saying that I've never had him knowingly lie to me. And I definitely don't think you're a ho. "

"So, are you anything like him, Max?"

"Like Jay? I don't think so, but he is my cousin and I do love him. He's family. "

" I don't need to be coming between you and anybody, Max."

"Glover, I've got a lot of crazy shit going on in my head about now. I know I said 'no strings' and stuff, but I would be a liar if I wasn't hoping that tonight would move us in another direction. I had no idea that 'this' would be the direction. You've got your life with Lionel and I've got mine, Glover. I think it's time the games end."

No words were spoken the rest of the way home. Max did give me a kiss on the cheek before I got out of the car. I told him that I didn't want to be walked to my door. I started walking toward my apartment when Max drove off, but then turned around when he got down the street. I decided to walk alone in the dark with my thoughts and tears. I thought about Max's "no strings" remark and about how I had avoided the word "love" with him. The funny thing was that I was silently hoping that tonight would move us in another direction as well.

44

Max

I was hurt and confused after the night ended. Jay had managed to push my buttons and I lashed out at Glover. Or *was* that how it went down? Was she playing me? That night was the first time my unwavering belief in what I thought I knew was shaken. Glover had dictated the terms since the beginning. In the beginning, she pulled my application and called me even though she was engaged. Then there was the other night when she showed up at my doorstep. I could have stopped everything at any one of those times, but I wasn't man enough. I liked the attention and her company. Hell, I liked her . . . and still do. Love was probably a more appropriate word, but I was too pissed to go there. To top everything off, I had come to blows with my cousin. Jay's venom-filled words were still smarting.

I was on my way to work Friday evening when I ran into Smitty on the parking lot. I hadn't seen my little buddy since our swap meet trip following the brawl in my apartment with Lionel. Smitty's ride was working and he had just pulled up. Smitty's job was starting to pay off for him. I could tell he had bought a bunch of white dress shirts and a few more ties to add to his work wardrobe. We gave each other dap as we passed each other.

"Max*well*, where ya at, boy!"

"Jus' chillin', Smit. How ya been?"

"Never better, man. Never better. At six months, I'll be up for a pay raise. Right now, I'm saving to get another ride. Heard anything yet with the jobs?"

"Nope. I'll give it another week before I start looking further out. I should spend the money on a computer. The Internet would come in handy right about now."

"Yeah. My cousin has one. 'Cept he uses it for those chat rooms. Fool stays up at night with a bunch of dudes pretendin' to be women and shit. If I can't see it, then I don't want to be with it. You haven't had any visitors lately, huh?"

"Naw. That was the only time he came around. If he comes back, I'll tell him to leave another hundred-dollar bill for you. That whole chapter is closed though . . . permanently."

"What??!! I *know* thangs ain't through between you and ol' girl. I thought I heard your little crackerjack stereo blastin' the other night. Fine ass Glover was there, huh?"

"Doesn't matter, man. All that shit is behind me now. I went home last weekend. Had to get away for a little while."

"Aww, dawg! I wanted to go see some of those high-yellow girls out there. You didn't think to ask me if I wanted to tag along?"

"It came up suddenly, my brother. I'll remember next time. Jay was screaming at me about that too."

"Where's Pretty-boy been lately?" Shit. I had to bring up Jay.

"At home, I guess. Saw him the other night. He's still the same." An asshole.

"Max, I'm off this Wednesday. I've been working late and they don't want to pay me more overtime. Wanna hit Venice?"

"That sounds good. You're still working on being the next Kobe, right?"

"Nah, dawg. Vince Carter. My game is evolving. I think my physical game is closer to his now."

"*Whatever*, Smit. I gotta run. Talk atcha later. "

The drive to Denny's was uneventful except for having to go back to get my apron that I forgot. The restaurant was more crowded than usual. A church bus was on the parking lot when I pulled up, so its passengers must have made up most of the customers. Staying busy was exactly what I needed. I tied my apron in back as I headed in the door. Samir was at work on the same shift with me for the first time this week. He was bringing some menus out to two elderly churchgoers.

"Glad you could make it, Max!" Samir shouted in his usual upbeat manner. By looking at the crowd, I could tell he *really* meant it.

I replied, "Samir, I'm glad I made it too!" And with that I strolled to the back with a smile on my face

45 _Glover_

I had made the twenty-six mile trip from Long Beach to Catalina a few times before, but never in a helicopter. I was feeling nervous about the ride. Every other time we had taken the trip by boat. As we drove down to the Port of Long Beach and past the surfer dudes, Lionel gave me the chance to chicken out, but I was all woman. As the Volvo pulled into the parking lot, I did clench Lionel's free hand a little harder. Lionel leaned over and gave me a kiss on the cheek to calm me down. I closed my eyes behind my tortoise shades and let my nervousness and doubt drift away.

I was wearing a short-sleeved white linen dress with tan sandals and my little straw hat. It was still morning time and the cool breeze made me wish I had worn something else. The helicopter ride wouldn't help. Lionel was wearing a tight blue shirt with gray slacks. His abs were showing through the fabric and the weather appeared not to bother him. His fake fashion spectacles were dangling on the end of his nose as we strolled toward the heliport. Lionel had 20/20 vision, but liked to go with the distinguished look from time to time.

It looked like we were going to have two fellow passengers on this cool Saturday morning. One was an elderly, balding white man with a camera around his neck. The other passenger was a middle-aged East Indian gentleman wearing a turban. We were greeted by the cheery flight crew and given our little safety

164

speech. We were then led to the bright yellow bird we were going to be riding in. Lionel spoke with the pilot who was waiting on us and told him we would need a taxi on the island. I still considered the boat trips to be more romantic, but the aerial view of L.A. Harbor and the island was breathtaking. It made me think of my dream where I was flying and fell into Max's arms. Yep. Yep. Yep. Time to think about other stuff.

The flight took about fifteen minutes, but it seemed to last longer than that. I guess I was taking in so much that time slowed for me. Lionel had wrapped his arms around me to keep me warm on the way out. When we landed on Catalina Island, our taxi was waiting to take us into town. Our wedding was going to be held at one of the inns on the island with the actual ceremony taking place up the canyon overlooking Catalina Bay and the Pacific Ocean. I expected Adele to make the trip with us, as she was the grande dame of preparations and such. Just my luck that she was already there when we arrived. Lionel's father, Goodwin Dunning Jr., was also there with the Mrs. I guess Lionel spoke with him and he was going to attempt to keep Adele in check. Mr. Dunning was simply an older version of Lionel, except for the salt and pepper hair and the fact that he was a few inches shorter. Both of Lionel's parents gave me a hug and a kiss when we walked up to the outdoor preparation area.

"Oh Glover, you are looking so pretty this morning! Carlo the fitter called me, you know. You are going to make such a lovely bride for my son. I was debating with Goodwin when you walked up. Do you think the orchestra should go here or over there?"

"I think it depends on the placement of the tables, Mrs. Du . . . Adele," I answered as I caught myself. I still wasn't calling the roody-poo bitch "mom".

"Well, we can decide that later. Have you heard from any of your people yet, Glover? I'm trying to get an informal head count for the caterer. It doesn't really matter. I'd rather err on the side of excess anyway."

"No, I haven't heard anything. There may be some friends from school, but I haven't heard from my relatives in Virginia."

Lionel's dad interjected, "Glover, I know it's late notice for them, but let me know if they need to be flown in. I'll take care of it if you don't have any problems with it." Lionel's dad was being helpful with no strings attached. I honestly felt like he had no problems with his son marrying a "commoner". He really went out of his way to make me feel like family.

I smiled and politely said, "Thank you, Mr. Dunning. I'll let you know." I didn't expect any of my relatives to show, but I wasn't going to admit it in front of Adele.

"Hey, Glover! Come take a look!" Lionel hollered in my direction. He had walked away from us and was admiring the view. I walked over beside him. The haze had burned off and we could see past the yachts in the bay and out into the never-ending blue.

"This is wonderful, Lionel. It makes me think about our first time out here."

"Good. This time will be the best ever. See out there? The doves will be flying out and turning around right there," Lionel said while gesturing toward a point in the sky.

"I can't wait."

"Glover . . . I'm glad you made this choice. I love you."

" . . . I love you too, Lionel."

46

Max

I had just hung up the phone when it rang. I was on earlier checking on movie times. I hadn't seen anything since sneaking out with Glover. This was gonna be a solo run this time.

"May I speak with Maxwell Guillory?"

"Yes, this is he."

"Mr. Guillory, this is Amy Sorinson with Sandifer Industries Human Resources Department. How are you today?"

"Fine, fine," I answered as I ran around the apartment looking for a pen and paper. I slipped on one of my tennis shoes, but regained my balance.

"Mr. Guillory, I am calling to inform you that we received your job search information from the State of California. We're in a partnership with the State. There were no current job matches available with the State, so they forwarded your information to us. Mr. Guillory, your employment application came with an impressive recommendation from your local Employment Development Office. Okay?"

"Okay." Glover. It had to be.

"Mr. Guillory, Sandifer Industries is headquartered in Concord, but we also have offices in the Greater Los Angeles area. Mr. Guillory, would you be interested in interviewing for one of our openings."

"Yes, I would. Could you tell me more about the position." I had located some paper and was fumbling around for a pen still.

"Good! Mr. Guillory, we have an opening for Human Resources Assistant in Concord as well as in Los Angeles. Sandifer

Industries is involved in the field of medical equipment sales and the interview would take place in Concord."

"Excuse me if I sound dumb, but where is Concord located? I'm not totally familiar with California." I had located a pen and was scribbling down the information.

"No sir, you don't sound dumb at all. Concord is located in northern California, northeast of Berkley and Oakland. Mr. Sandifer is a real "hands on" employer and he likes to meet potential employees personally. We will provide transportation and all additional information will be forwarded to you in a packet via certified mail. The salary range will be included and is open to discussion. We would like to schedule the interview as soon as possible and would appreciate your calling us with the date you have selected. Of course, this is after you have had a chance to review the packet material."

"Okay."

"And if you have a couple of minutes, I would like to confirm some personal information."

We continued talking for three more minutes. After I calmly turned the phone off and placed it on the counter, I erupted in a fit of joy. I ran around the living room jumping and pumping my fist. It was a scene from the NBA playoffs when Jordan hit the game winner against the Cavaliers except with no cameras. Okay, Jordan was missing from my apartment too. If all went as I hoped, then I would finally be on my way to some stability and opportunity in my life. I didn't know whether Glover's recommendation had any bearing on my call or consideration, but I wanted to call her and thank her anyway. I was lying to myself again. I just wanted to hear her voice one more time. I walked away from the phone. Getting out of town for the interview would do me some good. If I distracted myself a few weeks longer, Glover would be happily married and completely out of reach.

I called my mom to let her know about the upcoming interview. It was the first bit of positive news on the job front since moving and I needed to hit her with it as soon as possible. This kind of news would keep her "come back to Lake Charles" song at bay for at least until I had a serious job.

47 *Glover*

We weren't going to able to squeeze in some club hopping before my wedding, but we did manage to attend a step-aerobics class together Wednesday evening. Mona had a new membership and got me as well as Charmaine in on guest passes. Mona stood one row in front of us while we struggled in back to keep up. I wasn't as out of breath as Charmaine, but my coordination left something to be desired. This Chicano dude on the right of Charmaine struck up a winded conversation with her during class. He was a little short for my tastes, but this had nothing to do with me.

When the class was over, Charmaine and her new friend stopped by the wall following the cool-down. Ms. Mona and myself left for the juice bar. Mona ordered a cranberry juice for herself while I ordered a strawberry shake for Charmaine and a diet shake for myself. I had a wedding dress to fit into and didn't need any surprises on the big day. Charmaine strolled over to meet us at the table shortly afterwards. She was whistling so that meant she got the digits.

"Hey y'all! Mona's not the only person who can pick up someone in a gym!" Charmaine oozed as she pulled up a chair.

"Girl, leave me out of this. You know I don't pick up people; they just happen to gravitate in my direction. What's your new friend's name anyway?" Mona asked as she adjusted her black sports bra with one hand and looked at her hair in her compact mirror with the other.

"Yeah! Spill the beans, Ms. Fulda!" I egged Charmaine on.

Charmaine replied, "He told me his name was Rene', but ya never know. He probably came in here just to pick up on someone."

"And what did *you* come here for tonight?" Mona asked with one eyebrow raised. She had finished fixing her hair and was chuckling in amusement.

"For your information, Ms. Stevens, I came here tonight to bond with my friends and to whip my fat ass into shape. Most importantly, I came to spend some time with my dawg, G-love, before she gets hitched, moves to the 'burbs, and never sees us again."

"Aww, Charmaine. You know I'm not disappearing on y'all. I'll still be here and we'll be hangin' as always."

"Glover, you have any ideas about what you want to do after you're married? You must have some plans or dreams other than staying at the office with us," Mona added.

"Don't laugh, y'all. I've always wanted to own a business making gift baskets for people. That's something I would like to do at some point in life. I don't know how realistic it is, but it's always been a secret dream of mine."

"I think it's cool, G-love. I'm still plodding through life in a daze. What about you, Mona?"

"I don't know. I just don't know. As far as a career goes, I may go back to college one day. I think I've avoided moving up in salary intentionally. Deep down, I'm afraid of becoming like my dad. I'm not getting any younger, but to tell you the truth . . . I may never get married. I like my independence."

"So the diva likes to be a rebel," I said while sipping on my shake.

"It is the nature of a diva to be rebellious. I know these things."

"What *don't* you know, Mona," Charmaine joined in, "You might as well write a 'Diva for Dummies' book."

The table broke out in laughter. Mona had finished her drink and she threw her straw at Charmaine. It was times like this that I knew why I hung with my girls. Each one was crazy in her own way. I told myself things would be the same, but I didn't know what changes would come with marriage.

"Are you inviting any of our classmates from school?" Mona asked.

"Yeah. I sent invitations to Darnae and Sydeaka. Well, to the last addresses I had for them anyway. I also sent some to a couple of fellow Rams from my high school."

Mona giggled and replied, "Hmm. Sydeaka. That's a name I haven't heard in years."

"Charmaine, let me fill you in. You see, Mona and Sydeaka used to compete to outdress each other at college."

"And I won every time . . . almost. I'm in your wedding so she doesn't stand a chance this time either. Glover, you forgot to mention on the invitations that I'm in your wedding, huh?" There was silence around the table as Charmaine and I gave Mona blank stares.

"Mona, you're kidding, right?"

Mona sat there with a blank expression on her face and didn't answer me.

Charmaine asked next, "You are kidding, huh? About the invitations . . . "

Mona still sat there looking at us like we were stupid then said "Gotcha!"

48

Max

Venice Beach wasn't ready for us this time. The last time we'd balled here we lost both two-on-two games. We went out to Venice earlier this time. It was still cool and I didn't have to worry about cramping up. Smitty was glad to be off in the middle of the week because it reminded him of the old times when he had the crazy work schedule like me. Smitty was in his usual silly mood and stopped to listen to this crazy brother in a blonde wig. The man was wearing purple coveralls with yellow polka dots and was doing some corny rap routine that only tourists would find cute. Anyway, he and Smitty wound up getting into it. Smitty egged the fool on and then didn't want to leave any money in the guy's pink circus hat when the rap was finished.

We got away from the "fashion statement" and made it past the human biceps in the weight pit on our way to the basketball court. We had a short wait this time to get out on the court. The two dudes who beat us last time were there again. Didn't these guys have a job or something? I think they remembered us too by the way they started grinning when we walked up. This time, we wound up having a three-on-three with us picking this big ass "Q-dog" for our team. Some rollerbladers in bikinis had stopped to check out our game so we didn't want to disappoint. We got in three games this time with our rivals winning the first one, but with us taking the next two convincingly. Smitty's jumpshot was a little too sweet. I think he had been getting some playing time in on the D-L. I played much better this time also. I was using the game for stress relief and took my aggression to the hole along with the ball. Slam!

We congratulated each other and on the games well played and gave each other high-fives, but our two rivals were no longer smiling. They gave us the nod of respect though. Our team even got a few cheers from the women by the fence. They could have been yelling over our teammate's muscles he was flexing at them, but Smitty and me knew it was our game that had the women droolin'. Yeah, right. I placed my towel over my head as we walked off the court talking shit.

"Damn, dawg! You were up for it today, huh?" Smitty slapped me on the back.

"Hell yeah! I'm tired of being a victim, Smit. Nothing but wins from here on out."

"What's up with that, Max? Sounds like you're still tryin' to get Glover out
your system."

"Too late. She's already out. Did I tell you I got a job interview? Next week. Up in Concord. Wednesday."

"For real? Aww! That's my boy!" Smitty said as he stopped suddenly on the side of the walkway. "Looks like we're gonna be eatin' prime rib soon. Your treat, of course."

"Wish me luck, man. Salary starts in the fifties. I would be assisting with recruiting and hiring for this medical equipment company. I'll find out more when I go up there. I think Glover's recommendation helped when my application was turned in to the State."

"Sounds like you need to thank her. You guys make a cute couple, dawg and you normally don't hear that mushy kind of shit from me."

"I think the best way to thank her is to stay out of her life," I said as we continued walking.

"That sounds like some shit from a cheesy movie, but I guess you know what's best for you. What you need is a good piece of ass that'll make you move on . . . "

"Stop. If you're trying to do Zena favors and hook me up with Sonia still," I said as I shook my fist at Smitty.

"Man, I apologized for that already. Besides, Sonia moved on after she saw you all googly-eyed with Glover at the barbecue. She's hooked up with the brother that sold Zena her rims and shit."

"I haven't seen Zena around in a while. You guys still kickin' it?"

"Yeah. Sometimes. We've always done our own thing, but things are coolin' off, y'know. She's been acting distant since I got my job. I kinda expected it. I think she liked it better when I was broke. There's also some women at the job."

"*Oh?*"

"Nah. Nothing like that. I'm not about to get my ass fired. They're *foin* at West-tel, don't get me wrong, but Zena liked Home Stop better because less women worked there."

"Sounds like she likes controlling you, Smitty."

"She need to control all them damn lollipops she be suckin'. You hungry?"

"Hell yeah," I answered while looking at the food stand up ahead.

"Good, cause I see that polka dot fool coming through the crowd."

We sped up our pace and headed for the hotdogs.

49 *Glover*

I didn't realize how much junk I had until I tried to pack it up. I sat in the middle of my apartment floor in the same red Minnie Mouse sleep shirt I went to bed in the night before. Lionel would be by later to help bring some things to his, umm . . . our . . . the house. I skipped hanging out and went to bed early Friday night. I eyeballed what things I wanted to box up before getting some shuteye and put everything into action at the crack of dawn. My lease expired at the end of the month, but I would be married before then. My furniture was going into storage until I figured out what to do with it. That would be sometime after our honeymoon.

We were honeymooning in Zimbabwe at Victoria Falls. Lionel's mother tried to talk us into going to Athens, Greece, but we would always have time to take a regular trip there. To hell with her. Adele's baby boy was taking his Queen to see Africa for her honeymoon.

I had a large green garbage bag half-filled with stuff I was throwing out. From all the junk I'd hoarded and accumulated, I knew there were going to be several more bags to take out to the dumpster on the parking lot. I was trying to decide what I felt like fixing for breakfast when my phone rang. I assumed it was Lionel. I crawled over a stack of old magazines and located my phone. I was lying on my back with my legs crossed when I answered.

"I thought your ass would. be here by now. You know it's wrong to keep your bride-to-be waiting."

"Hello?" Oops. The voice on the other end was confused and it definitely wasn't Lionel.

I caught myself and said, "Yes?"

"Is that you Glover?" The voice sounded familiar, like something from a distant memory.

While trying to place the voice, I answered, "Yes. May I ask who's calling?"

"It's your Uncle Robert."

Robert. That name brought back a few memories. Robert was my mother's half-brother. I assumed he was still in Virginia. I had met him once or twice while visiting at my maw-maw's as a little kid. Robert was mostly a loner and kept to himself. I think he was keeping up my grandmother's house since she passed away. I had sent an invitation addressed to him there.

"Uncle Robert? Hey! How are you??!!"

"I'm making it, my niece. We're all doing fine out here. Look, we got your invitation and I just had to call you. I called the RSVP number and spoke with this woman . . ."

"Adele?"

"Yeah! That's it! That's your mother-in-law, right? Nice woman. She spoke very highly of you, Glover. We talked for a good while. Anyway, she gave me your number so I could call you." Shit. She was probably pumping Uncle Robert for information on our family. Lionel's mom could be the charmer. "I know we haven't been close, but I was so happy about your wedding when the invitation came in the mail. Y'know, I'm married now myself."

"For real?"

"Yep. Your Uncle Robert slowed down long ago. Got a wife and two little kids now. Working up at the factory too."

"Aww! I'd love to see you again and meet your family as well."

"Well, you'll get your wish. We're coming to your wedding, Glover. More of your people wanted to go out there to California, but didn't have enough time to take off from work and stuff."

"Well, I'm sorry about that. That's all my fault, Uncle Robert. Look, I don't want to inconvenience you or put you guys out. I'll understand if you can't attend."

"No, no. I've got some money saved up and my wife has been wanting to see the West Coast. We're coming to see our girl off properly, that is, unless you don't want us there."

"No! No! Not at all. I want to see you and I would be honored to have you at my wedding."

"Thank you, niece. Glover, you know your momma and me were never that close. God rest her soul. I just want to let you know that I regret that to this day. You know how most of our family is. People get caught up in doin' their own thangs and it winds up being years before anybody speaks again. I've been probably the worst of them all. I also want to let you know that I'm sorry and that maybe we can make a change." My uncle's words were never so true.

"Yeah. Maybe we can, Uncle Rob," I replied as a lump formed in the back of my throat.

"You're going to make a lovely bride. Girl, last time I saw you; you were the spitting image of your momma except for those eyes. Those eyes you got from your dad. Heh. *Worthless bum.* Sorry about that."

"Uncle Rob?"

"Yeah, Glover?"

"Umm, I know it's late notice and all and I will understand if you say, 'No', but I was wondering . . . if would you walk me down the aisle?"

"Of course, niece. "

From a better place, my mother was smiling.

50   *Max*

My airline tickets came with complete instructions on how to get to Sandifer Industries. I wore my brown suit pants, brown loafers and my white T-shirt for the flight from LAX to Oakland International. I carried my shirt, coat, and red silk tie in a small garment bag, as I wanted to be at least partially fresh for my interview. When I landed in Oakland that morning, I was to look for the BART. I didn't know what it was, but decided to worry about that after changing. I found a restroom and finished changing into my interview suit. I folded my garment bag up tightly and stored it in my briefcase. I had two hours before my interview and still had to negotiate my way from Oakland to Concord.

I bought the ticket needed and followed the signs to the BART. I discovered that the BART was a high-speed electric train system. When I first heard the name, I had incorrectly guessed that it was a freeway or bus. I was just getting used to Los Angeles but was walking around here like a tourist. If I wound up getting this job, I would probably become more familiar with the Bay Area.

As I rode the train north to the City Center station, I took the time to peek at my mini map of the area. It was going to take only thirty minutes from City Center to Concord based on my papers. Since I had a little time, I decided to skip the first train to Concord. The trains were running roughly every half-hour so I decided to unwind a little and scope out the place.

Goosebumps were popping up on my arms and neck as I stood in the crowd of people moving here and there. The same thing happened when I first moved to L.A. The thrill of a new challenge and new place gave me a nervous feeling, but a "good" nervous feeling. I tried to envision this as the first day of my professional career as I stood there in my suit and inhaled deeply. I envisioned the same thing before when I stood in the CBD of downtown L.A., but the feeling was stronger this time. I felt surer that I belonged in this world. I wanted to stretch my arms out and proclaim myself "King of the World" like Leonardo DiCaprio, but decided against it. I didn't have a job yet and didn't need to be beat down and carted off by Oakland PD.

My confidence carried me from Oakland to Concord. From the BART train to the taxicab that took me through the manicured main gate of Sandifer Industries, it was with me. I admired the landscaping on the grounds as my cabby droned on with the history of Concord, California and Sandifer. I probably should have paid attention, but I was daydreaming about someone playing golf on the grass at this place. The only thing that stuck was him saying that Concord used to be called "All Saints" by the Spanish, but that was it.

We entered a large circular drive and came around the Sandifer logo in front of the headquarters main entrance. I gave the cabby a very generous tip and hoped that I would recoup the money soon with a first paycheck. The building was only five stories tall, but the shiny metal and glass front stretched on forever. A security guard guided me in to the front desk where I was given a visitors badge. I was early for my interview so I asked for a restroom. I opened my briefcase and reapplied some cologne, did the breath and underarm checks, and eyed myself out in the mirror before taking the elevator up to the fifth floor.

I adjusted my suit in the elevator on the way up and became conscious of every little wrinkle and line in my suit. "Just breathe," I thought to myself as the pinging sound indicated I had arrived at my destination. A bearded white guy in a light blue button-down shirt with khaki pants greeted me. He introduced himself as 'Brad' and I assumed he was from HR as he escorted me down the hall. We talked some small talk and he offered to get me a drink as we walked. We stopped at a corner office at the end of a long corridor, which had a plaque on the door. I scanned the words as I was led in through the massive door. They read "Bradley Sandifer III". An HR rep was in the interview, but my guide was not the person. This was the president of the company who was walking with me. I was sooo glad I didn't do or say anything stupid.

The interview was conducted by both of them with Brad doing most of the talking. The HR rep sat and made notes while joining in from time to time. I felt pretty comfortable in the interview and I hoped that it was reflected in my answers. The president, Brad, was an energetic kind of fellow and seemed to be straight out of an infomercial at times as he explained the business and the products. The only uncomfortable moment in the interview was when my pager started vibrating. This happened in the middle of the interview and I chose to ignore it. By the time the interview had ended, I had forgotten all about it.

Following the interview, Brad gave me a brief tour of Sandifer Industries headquarters. I was given the impression that I had the job pending my physical and drug test, which I wasn't worrying about. I had always been straightlaced when it came to drugs anyway. Salary still had to be discussed and agreed upon as well. Brad was unsure if the opening would be in the Bay Area or L.A., but I wasn't too picky with an opportunity like this. Maybe a change of scenery would do me good as Glover's face and the feel of her skin was still on my mind. This was even after all the craziness with Jay. I was still wrestling with the issue of who was telling the truth, but it didn't matter since any chance with Glover was kaput. She was jumping the broom this weekend if I remembered correctly.

As I was heading out to the front lobby, I asked the receptionist if I could borrow the phone. I would be flying back to L.A. in about four hours and needed to call a cab as well as check my messages at home. I made a mental note to buy a cell phone when I got home. I called a cab first then used my calling card to make the long distance call to L.A.

My answering machine told me I had two messages. The first message began playing when I remembered my page. I was looking down at the displayed number I didn't recognize when I heard the message.

"Max, this is your Aunt Verna, baby. I need you to call us as soon as possible. Something's happened to your cousin. Junior's been shot." Aunt Verna's voice was shaky and tearful.

I stood there at the desk in shock. I felt weak in the knees and took a deep breath as I hung up. I didn't bother waiting to hear the second message. I started dialing their number in Carson directly without using my calling card when I stopped. Something told me to try the number on my pager. I began dialing the number, but put in the 310 area code first. The phone rang a few times, then it was answered.

"UCLA Medical Center."

51 *Glover*

Most of my recent nights were spent at Lionel's home going over last minute wedding details. I had taken leave from my job, as the wedding plans needed to be finalized. I apologized to Lionel's father for my Uncle Rob replacing him in the wedding. An apology really wasn't needed, but I felt obliged, as Goodwin had been very kind to me throughout this. Uncle Rob had his measurements taken at a tux shop in Virginia and called them in to me. He and his family would be here Friday and I offered my apartment to them since I still had a few weeks on the lease. I would just hold off on moving my furniture. It was going to feel good having family at my wedding. Deep, deep down it still didn't feel totally right, but there was no turning back.

Sigh. I was going to miss the place. A lot of my belongings were moved or packed up now. My cozy, cluttered apartment was starting feel vanilla and empty. I had lived here the last five years and a lot of my personality went into my home. From the odd picture frames to the little green ceramic frogs in my bathroom, this place had been me.

Most of my stuff didn't fit with the theme of my future home. I entertained the thought of setting up a little private room to myself over there, a place where I could escape and be me. I dismissed that idea as being childish and immature. Fuck it.

Lionel would just have to put up with my little frogs in the bathroom. It still wasn't real for me, but it would do.

My last piece of unfinished business needed to be taken care of. I could only do it alone and in the privacy of my apartment. I picked up the phone several times before putting it back down on the stand and walking away. I even let out a shriek of frustration as I kicked one of my throw pillows across the floor. I was terrified that someone would answer and my cool would disintegrate. Yep. I was being one trifling sister right about now. After pulling enough of my hair out, I went for it. The phone rang as I stood there with my eyes closed. I was praying that the answering machine would pick up instead and my wish was granted. I kept my eyes closed and let my thoughts come out.

"Max, it's me. You probably didn't expect to hear from me again and you may not want to hear from me."

I kept my eyes closed and bit my lip before continuing.

"Don't worry. This is the last time you'll hear my voice. I'm through fucking up your life."

I exhaled deeply.

"There's just stuff I need to get off my chest and I don't trust myself talking directly to you. As strong as I believe myself to be, I . . . guess I'm a scared little girl deep down. More like a coward, the more I think about it."

"I've done some awful shit since first meeting you. I've schemed and given into temptation . . . and liked it. I've done some wrong things to both you and my fiancé."

I let out a nervous giggle as I prepared to bare my soul to a lifeless machine even more.

"Max, for that shit that went down with your cousin . . . I don't blame you for believing him even if you say you don't. As misguided as your loyalty may be to him, it is loyalty that you have. That's probably one of the things I like about you, your prehistoric sense of honor. Loyalty is something that . . . that I've been lacking. I'm trying to make up for that."

I paused as I debated whether to continue. I was hoping that the tape would end and the phone would hang up on me.

"Max, we've never said the words, but Lionel knows or suspects what was going on with us. I don't have to tell you that though. I'm sorry for that going down. I'll have to live with what I've done and with what I'm about to say . . ."

My heart was screaming out for the first time since my mother had passed away. Tears were waiting to burst forth, but I wouldn't let them.

"I love you, Max." Four simple words that felt like a ton off my shoulders once spoken.

"Heh. I think I realized it when we first had lunch at the diner. Oh God . . . I can't believe I admitted this." I was getting choked up and my words were slowing.

"I love you enough that I want nothing but happiness for you with whoever is lucky enough to be yours and yours alone. I wish it were me, but unfortunately, it can't be. Max . . . I will never speak these words to you again . . . or even admit saying them. Max, it was nice knowing you for this brief time. Don't even think about calling me because I won't be here. I'll be married this weekend. I'm sorry for everything . . . Goodbye, Max."

I didn't open my eyes for several minutes after hanging up. The flood walls were holding tears back, but I refused to cry. I was Glover, my mom's tough little girl. I then unplugged the phone from the wall and left.

52

Max

I didn't like the silence in ICU. On any other floor, it would have been cool. Here, it reminded me of death. Bells, whistles, laughter, anything would have be welcome. Aunt Verna's wailing shattered the silence. I rushed around the corner to see Aunt Verna going ballistic. Uncle Mo was holding her tightly and was rocking back and forth to soothe her. They were standing in the hallway outside a room. I assumed it was Jay's by the position they took in front of it. The two of them stood there as if protecting the room from some unseen threat. I slowed as I came up on them and waited to make eye contact. The look of relief on my Aunt and Uncle's faces told me the most important thing; Jay was still alive. Aunt Verna was still crying. Her eyes were painfully swollen and the salt from her tears was dried on her cheeks. Uncle Mo was being the rock of the family. His eyes were red and his voice sounded strained as he greeted me. We all embraced in silence for minutes.

Aunt Verna did her best to fill me in when I had called the hospital earlier. Jay had been shot last night. He took two in the back after work. He was on the mall parking lot with some woman when her baby's father came up from behind and shot him. The guy ran off and left Jay bleeding on the ground with two nine millimeter slugs in him. The son of a bitch was still on the loose when we had talked. It was touch and go most of the night, but they got Jay stabilized just before dawn. Aunt Verna had left a message on my answering machine this morning, but I had already left for the airport. Uncle Mo found my number and had paged me when they didn't hear from me. I was about to receive some more news.

"Maxwell, your cousin done it this time. Messin' with them girls finally caught up with him. I told him time and time again, but his ass wouldn't listen," Uncle Mo said as he cleared his throat.

"I'm sorry I couldn't be here sooner. Is . . . is he gonna be alright, Uncle Mo?"

Aunt Verna composed herself and answered, "Junior had his spleen taken out. He . . . he can't feel his legs, Max." Aunt Verna broke down once again.

"The doctor just told us about his legs when you got here. My . . . my boy might be paralyzed. If I catch the punk that did this, I will kill his ass." Uncle Mo's voice broke off as he covered his face with his hands and lost it as well.

Uncle Mo's hard, manly cry rocked me to my core. One of them, I could handle but not both. I started losing it too as I tried to tend to them. A petite nurse came out from the nurses' station to help and sat down with my aunt. The nurse told my aunt that God was going to take care of everything and rubbed Aunt Verna's back.

A doctor and another nurse came out of Jay's room just then. Jay was stable and conscious, but in a lot of pain. One of the slugs was still in him and it wouldn't be known if the paralysis was permanent until after the swelling had gone down. The doctor told me that Jay was asking for me, but to make my visit short. I was caught off guard by Jay's request, especially after our last incident. I don't think my aunt and uncle knew anything about that. I gave a smile to them as I wiped my face and entered the room. Aunt Verna had located her rosary in her purse and her lips were moving in prayer as my eyes turned toward Jay's room door.

Jay's eyes were closed and flickering as I approached. His face looked dry and pale and he had tubes in his arms and nose. My gaze trailed down to his legs out of instinct. I was hoping to see a twitch or something.

"Whaddup, cuz?" came from Jay's mouth. His voice

sounded frog-like and his lips barely moved.

"Hey. Don't talk too much, man."

"Moms okay?"

"Yeah. She's in the hall with Uncle Mo."

"*Cough. Cough.* Sit down, Country. I gotta talk to you . . . " I thought Jay had drifted back asleep until he motioned toward the chair on the side of his bed. I sat down and pulled the chair closer.

"Remember when I dropped out of school?"

"Yeah."

"I gotta tell you about that."

Jay went on and slowly told me about how he was when he got to UCLA. Jay was the same old Jay that I've always known. He was the wild womanizer he was to this day. He went on to tell me about when that all changed in his second year. Jay met Mrs. Right at the library one day and fell madly in love with her. No one off campus knew about this though, not even my aunt and uncle. They dated for two semesters and were inseparable. Jay had given up all his playing and was going to propose to her. Jay had bought a ring and planned to move out of Uncle Mo's. One day, Jay had the ring with him and had popped by her apartment to surprise her and got a surprise he wasn't expecting. Jay had been played. The girl was seeing Jay as well as one of the brothers on the football team and this white dude. And she was fucking all of them. The worse part was that the whole campus knew she was playing Jay and he was the only one in the dark. Jay wound up throwing the ring at her and walking away. Jay told me that he changed from that point on. Jay never wanted to feel that kind of pain and humiliation again. He went back to his old ways, but was even worse. He was harder and more ruthless in the way he treated women. He wanted to pay that girl back in every other woman he messed with from that point on. Jay went on to say how he hated himself as well. That was when he left school and dropped out. Jay played every woman he had met since then out of insecurity. I think his playing finally caught up with him. I prayed that Jay would make a full recovery.

Jay went quiet again after his confession. I think he had fallen asleep. I sat there digesting everything. Damn. Jay was in love once upon a time and *nobody* knew. He was human. I guess his near-death experience made him want to get that off his chest. The nurse came in to check on Jay and I got up to leave. My hand was on the door handle when I heard Jay's voice again.

"I'm sorry, cuz." Not being sure of what I heard, I stopped dead in my tracks. His voice was still very low.

"Jay?" I said in his direction. I wasn't certain that he was awake.

"I'm sorry, cuz," came from Jay again. "I lied, man."

"What?"

"*Cough.* That girl, Glover. I made that shit up."

I stood there in stunned silence.

Jay continued, "I met her ass in the club, but she wouldn't give me any play. *Cough. Cough.* My pride was hurt, I guess. Maybe I was jealous when I saw her with you. Shit. I dunno."

"Dammit, Jay!" I reacted loudly. I caught myself when I looked at the monitor Jay was hooked up to. The nurse was surprised by my outburst, but then went back to pretending to ignore our conversation.

"I guess I was dumping a lot of my baggage on you when I said all that shit about her. Heh. Good punch, nigga. *Cough.* I'm sorry though. You always been the 'goody-two-shoes mutherfucker' in the family, Country. I got no right to hate on you."

I was fuming still, but it was dying down. "Don't worry about it, cuz. You just concentrate on getting better. That's all over with now anyway."

"*Cough. Cough.* Now you fuckin' with *me*, nigga. You in love with her. I knew that from the look on your face that night. That's why I was so mad . . . I *knew* that look. It was the same look I had before. You wouldn't have hit me like you did if you weren't in love."

"No, no. She's getting married. It's over, Jay."

"For real? Damn. I fucked shit up . . . Max?"

"Yeah?"

"Talk to her. If you do anything . . . do that." Jay fell back into unconsciousness.

The nurse then told me it was time to leave. I found out in the hallway that the shooter had been caught by LAPD.

53

Glover

Early Friday morning brought Lionel and me to LAX. My Uncle Robert and his family were in from Virginia and we made the drive there in a minivan. Lionel had rented it for Uncle Rob and them to use. He figured they would like the extra space and might want to do some sightseeing while in California. Uncle Rob's wife wasn't going to let him get out of here without hitting the tourist stops.

Uncle Rob and his family were waiting on us by passenger pickup. I still remembered what he looked like, but he was developing a little gut now. I spotted Uncle Rob right away because of the Howard University T-shirt he was wearing. Uncle Rob used to do maintenance work there and I saw that he still loved him some Howard. His wife, Tasha, was at his side. Her braids were sticking out from beneath her denim baseball cap. Tasha was chewing gum and talking to Uncle Rob while holding the children's hands. She and the kids were wearing T-shirts and shorts, but their shirts were obviously purchased here. The two women, Tasha and her daughter Tandy, were wearing Lakers T-shirts, but the little boy, Randy was wearing a Clippers T-shirt. Sigh. He was only three so I could excuse it. He probably liked the colors.

It brought so many memories rushing back from my trips to Virginia while listening to my uncle and his family during the ride to my apartment. This was my first time meeting Tasha, but she felt like family right off. Her manner was so

189

down-to-earth and she was funny as hell. She and Charmaine would make the wedding very memorable. We planned on letting the family unwind first at my apartment, since the dinner/rehearsal was later that evening, but they were ready to go. Uncle Rob and them wanted to eat at Roscoe's so we headed there after unloading their luggage at my place. I had moved most of my stuff over to Lionel's and was going to give them some privacy.

I still had some things to take care of before the rehearsal so we left the van with Uncle Rob for the rest of the day. I had a map of the area with some directions to different things for them, but Tasha was one step ahead of me. She had a highlighted map. We took some pictures for their photo album before Lionel and me left in my Civic.

"That was so sweet of you to rent the van for them," I said to Lionel with an appreciative smile as we drove off. I leaned over and gave him a kiss on the cheek. Lionel pretended to blush.

"Nothing to it, baby. I'm glad some of your family could make it. After all, they're going to be my family too in a couple of days."

"Yeah. One big, happy family."

The dinner/rehearsal was held at Lionel's parents' home that night. My uncle and his family followed Lionel and me over there. I watched the reaction of Uncle Rob and them in the rearview mirror as we drove through the gate. I smiled as I had the same reaction when I first came here. Rosa escorted us to the enormous glass-walled room in back. Rosa didn't disappear back up the hallway this time. She mingled in with the extra servants that were on hand for the night. The other members of the wedding party were already in attendance: Lionel's sister, Sarabeth; his cousins, Jacob and Jazelle; his co-worker Derek; Leu, his friend from Stanford; and Esai, this Dominican brother who's been friends with Lionel since childhood. Of course, my girls, Mona and Charmaine, were also there and lighting it up with their presence.

It was different seeing the large space filled with people, tables, and food. Even with everything in here, there was still enough room to hold the wedding in this place. Adele coordinated a brief run-through/rehearsal of what was to be expected on the island once she had everybody's attention. The wedding party was going to take the boat out to Catalina tomorrow for a walk-through at the inn and would spend the night there. The guests and other family would be ferried in for the ceremony on Sunday.

Following the dinner, the obligatory mingling took place. The noise of chatter and piano music filled the Dunning home. I met Lionel's buddies, but left them shortly so they could indulge in male bonding. Adele had a group in her clutches as she stood in the center of a circle on one end of the room. Goodwin had stepped out to smoke one of his Cuban cigars. Uncle Rob and Tasha were still seated, as the kids wanted more to eat, so I decided to hang out with them later. I was by the glass wall trying to see out into the night when I was tapped on the shoulder. Mona and Charmaine had found me.

"I done died and gone to heaven, y'all. You think your mother-in-law would give us a tour of the rest of the place, Glover?"

"Probably not. She's busy right now doing her thang for her audience."

"She's right, Glover. This is sweet. My father's house down the street is nothing to sneeze at, but the square footage here is colossal," Mona joined in as she lifted her glass up in an imaginary toast to the house itself. "Enough about the house. How are you managing tonight, Ms. McDaniel?"

"I'm doing alright, sistah," I answered as we lightly touched fists. "I don't know what I'd do if you two weren't here."

"We got your back as always, G-love," Charmaine assured me.

"I know, y'all. Part of me still wants to run out of here, y'know. I guess it's jitter time."

"You wouldn't be human if you didn't get the jitters. Now, a diva like me couldn't be caught having jitters."

"You mean an 'ice queen' like you, Mona?" Charmaine said while looking cross-eyed at her.

"Keep up that shit and your eyes are going to stick just like that," Mona replied as she playfully shoved Charmaine. "Seriously though, you are going to make a beautiful bride and an incredible wife and we both are sooo happy for you."

"Thanks, you two . . . for everything."

As I smiled, I looked back out the glass and into the darkness. The darkness was broken up by little dots of city lights. I picked one spot of light and focused on it. My eyes closed and my mind took me there.

54 *Max*

It was Friday evening when I realized that I had been wearing the same clothes since Wednesday. I took a whiff under my arms as I unlocked my apartment door and quickly put my arm down. Bad idea. I was filthy and needed my bed more than ever. I stayed at the hospital with Uncle Mo and Aunt Verna until they had chased me out of there. Jay still wasn't out of the woods completely, but he was much better than when he was carted into the joint. There still was no feeling in his legs and we were praying for that to change. I was still smarting from Jay's little talk with me, but it didn't matter just then. Jay's life was more important than any hurt or anger that was lingering in my heart.

I remembered to call Samir from the hospital and filled him in on the news, both good and bad, that had come up all in one day. He told me to take off whatever time I needed and to let him know how Jay was progressing. He congratulated me on the good interview and laughed as he told me to call him when he needed to hire another great worker. Samir was always more optimistic about my future than I was. It was time I shared that optimism and to generate a manly dose of it myself.

I pried my wrinkled suit off me and left it on the side of the hamper. It needed a serious dry cleaning and I needed a good scrubbing. The hot shower helped release the knotted muscles in my back. My back was telling me that sleeping in hospital chairs was something I didn't want to master. Sleep came calling on me as the steam rose up and filled the bathroom. It was time for me to answer its call before I wound up snoozing in the tub. I staggered out of the shower, toweled off and was asleep before my head hit the pillow. Clothes would have to wait.

My mind was racing as I slept. It was attempting to process everything from its whirlwind tour of interviews, gunshots, and revelations. Images of Oakland, Concord, and L.A. all blended together. Jay was standing over me and crying one moment and laughing the next. I was in the hospital bed all of a sudden with Lionel and Glover standing at the foot of the bed. A minister was standing at their side as they kissed. I tried to fly out of the bed to stop them, but fell down onto the floor. My legs wouldn't work and felt like rocks. Lionel kept kissing Glover only to stop to look down at me and smile. Glover would turn her head to look at me, but wouldn't say anything. She just gave me a sad look before she turned back to continue her kiss with Lionel. I tried to drag myself toward them but was unable. The world started slowing down until I felt a sharp pain. Somebody's foot was stamping on my hand. My eyes traveled upward to see who's foot it was.

I looked up to see Mr. Thomas, my barber from Lake Charles, standing there yelling at me. I couldn't understand a word he was saying at first, but the words became clearer as I concentrated. He was screaming, "Walk, boy! Walk!" I looked back toward Lionel and Glover. They were still there kissing, but Glover's image had begun to flicker and fade and in and out, like something off TV. I looked back up at Mr. Thomas and he nodded at me. I stretched my arm up and grasped the bed railing. Mr. Thomas disappeared as soon as my hand touched the bare metal. I grasped the railing with my other hand and began to pull myself up. I still couldn't feel my legs and almost slipped back down onto the floor, but something changed. Mr. Thomas was gone, but I was standing there now. Another me was there and screaming, "Walk, boy! Walk!" just as Mr. Thomas had done before. The clothes were nothing like I would have worn. They were older . . . like what my dad used to wear. I turned my attention back to Lionel and Glover and began pulling myself rung by rung along the side of the bed. Glover was still fading in and out, but her image was a lot blurrier. I started feeling sensation returning to my legs and fought to stand. The chant of "Walk, boy! Walk!" was getting stronger as my other self got in my face. There was a second of eye contact where something went on between my other self and me. There was an understanding where there was none before. The other me nodded, stepped back, and disappeared.

That left me alone and standing with Lionel, Glover, and the minister straight ahead. I cracked a smile as I began moving steadily toward them. Glover's image had blurred so much that I couldn't make her out. She was still kissing Lionel though. My slow movements began increasing as I prepared to leap at them. I was flying across the room at them when Glover's blurry image cleared up. Glover was no longer there. Someone else had replaced her. Lionel still was there, but he was kissing the new person now . . ."

The phone awakened me in mid-leap. I lay there naked across the bed with my eyes blinking.

The phone rang a few more times before I got my bearings and sat up. I didn't know how long I had been asleep.

"Hello?"

"Max, you okay, baby?" I felt strange as hell talking to my mom on the phone while naked.

"Um, yeah. I'm fine. Just getting some sleep. Been at the hospital . . . *yawn* . . . since Wednesday. Jay's doing better, Mom."

"Your Uncle Maurice told me. He called me from the hospital a little while ago. I told him to call any time. He said how tired you were and I wanted to make sure you made it back okay."

"Yeah. I made it, Mom. Mom? You ever think about Dad?"

"All the time, baby. All the time. But he exists in you, son. You know that, right?"

" . . . Yeah. I guess I do know that."

I finished my conversation with my mom and managed to throw on a pair of boxers. I tried to write the dream off as the product of a sleep-deprived mind. The answering machine showed two messages on it. I decided to check them before falling back asleep. I didn't need roller coaster dreams again

195

although I was still trying to make sense of it all. The first message was from Aunt Verna. She must have called me twice as I had heard the first one while at my interview. The second message was left on Wednesday also. I was rubbing my eyes when I heard Glover's voice.

"*Max, it's me.*"

Twenty minutes later, my Celica was speeding down San Vicente to Glover's apartment. I tried calling her number before running out my apartment, but it had been disconnected with no new number. I didn't see Glover's car on the parking lot, but that didn't stop me from pounding on her door until my knuckles hurt. She was out there somewhere. I just didn't know if I was going to have enough time to say or do anything.

55
Glover

The hum of the motor and the subtle rocking of the boat didn't help my hangover. I sat motionless with my legs up on the bench and my back resting against Lionel's shoulder. Those of us in the wedding party were going over to the inn on the island. Adele had gone over via helicopter at the crack of dawn. I didn't know where she got the energy. That was one thing I could admire about her, that and the fact that she gave birth to such a fine man as Lionel. Uncle Rob was sitting down the bench from me. He found out the boat ride was going to take over an hour and was in dreamland five minutes into the trip. At least there were no bugs around this morning to collect in his open mouth. Charmaine was playing on the upper decks with Uncle Rob and Tasha's kids. She was going to make a good mother one day. That freed Tasha up to snap some more photos. Tasha was out by the railing taking pictures of the Channel and the shore. Earlier, her ass took a bad picture of me over my objections. She was family so I excused it. Besides, I could always bribe the photo off her later for some Roscoe's.

"I'm having trouble keeping my hands off you, baby," Lionel said in my ear as he leaned his head against mine.

I adjusted my hat and playfully replied, "Baby, this pre-wedding abstinence must be kicking your ass, huh?"

"Yep. Bad idea. And I was the foolish one to suggest it last week. Haha."

Tasha woke up Uncle Rob prior to docking then the kids jumped in his lap. Mona had walked up from hiding and stood before us.

"Your big day is almost here, Ms. McDaniel. Yours too, Mr. Dunning," Mona said with her attention now focused on Lionel. "Treat my girl right, . . . okay?" Mona's eyes didn't blink.

"Of course, Mona. Would you think otherwise?" Lionel returned the same stare.

The strange little interchange between Mona and Lionel caught my attention, before it shifted to the docking announcement.

Upon docking, we spilled out into the town of Avalon on the island. Our bags and accessories were being delivered straight to the inn and Uncle Rob went with them. He had to have a last minute adjustment made in his tux, as the sleeves were too short.

He had commented to me, "Girl, this is Saks Fifth Avenue. I may never wear any of their stuff again. I want to be looking right."

Lionel and Leu were mumbling about golf to themselves as they discussed the courses on the island. We all had time for some sight seeing before the walk-through at the inn, so I excused Lionel so he could run off to the links for a "look see" with Leu. Esai left with the two of them and Derek, Lionel's co-worker, decided to shop for souvenirs. Lionel's best man, Jacob, who appeared to be smitten with Mona, lingered for a while before following the other three to the golf course. Jazelle, Jacob's twin sister, was sleepy from her Aunt Adele's party the night before so she gave me a hug and kiss on the cheek before excusing herself for a catnap.

That left me with Mona, Charmaine, Tasha and the kids, and Lionel's sister, Sarabeth.

I had never really gotten to know Sarabeth during my relationship with Lionel. She had spent most of that time abroad in Europe and would fly in for holidays. Just as Lionel shared his dad's complexion, Sarabeth shared her complexion with her mom. Sarabeth was an exotic beauty with an almond complexion and deep penetrating eyes. She wore her black hair long and straight, just like her build. Sarabeth was not one of many words except for those she was close to. I was feeling that I would probably never be in that category. My thoughts about her mom, the matriarch of the family, didn't help the situation.

As our group walked along, I tried to break the ice with my "sister-in-law".

"So what have you been doing in Europe, Sarabeth?"

"A little of this, a little of that. You know, one can never be too grounded out there."

"Heh. I wouldn't know. Never been there."

"*Oh*? That's right. I had forgotten. Lionel told me that before. You work at the *unemployment* office, right?"

"*The Employment Development Office* is the actual name of the place."

"Riiight," the bitch said with a dismissive smile. "So, are you quitting there before or after you go to Greece."

"I don't know if I am quitting. And it's Africa we're going to, not Greece."

"Yes. Silly me. Lionel told me about that change of plans. My mother was quite upset."

"Lionel tells you a lot, huh?"

Sarabeth stopped in mid-step. "Glover, my brother tells me *everything*." Her body language as well as her eyes reaffirmed that remark. I knew what she meant. At least I knew where I stood.

Sarabeth took that time to dismiss herself under the pretext of wanting to be fresh for the walk-through. She gave a parting smile to all of us then headed through the crowd to the inn.

"Bitch act like she got a worm up her ass," came from someone's mouth in our group. I looked at Charmaine who was dumbfounded. Someone had stolen her thunder with that comment. It was Tasha. She definitely fit in with Mona, Charmaine and me. The three of us erupted in laughter as we welcomed her to the three amigas.

Our walk-through took place on time up the canyon from the inn. The orchestra was there a day early and assisting the grounds crew with assembling their stand. The doves were already on the island as well. It looked like it wanted to rain, but we were lucky so far. The chance of rain was less for the wedding day.

Lionel stood in the front by the cliff overlooking the bay, while the coordinator called out instructions. Lionel's dad walked his mother up first. They then took their places in the first row of chairs. Next came Jacob walking up the main aisle holding Mona's hand. Charmaine and I both giggled, as we knew Jacob was about to have either a heart attack or bust a nut from being so close to Mona. Charmaine went next with Esai. It was only rehearsal, but Charmaine was working it down the aisle. I was so glad music wasn't playing. Leu was preparing to walk next and took Sarabeth's hand. Sarabeth took a brief second to look back at me before they began. The coordinator was running around and positioning people on their marks and paused the mock procession. As Derek and Jazelle got into position to begin their walk, I lined up nervously alongside Uncle Rob. My stomach was beginning to do back flips. Uncle Rob saw my change and calmly held my hand.

"Thank you, niece."

"For what?"

"Just for allowing me and my family into your life." Uncle Rob nodded toward the family. Tasha, Tandy, and Randy were sitting in one of the back rows near us and were waving up a storm.

I smiled at Uncle Rob and said, "I owe you." My stomach had calmed and it was our time to walk up.

56 *Max*

"You did what??!!"

Smitty stared at me like I was insane. He then tried to turn his Shaft music down with the remote. The remote wasn't working so he dropped it and ran over to the stereo while cursing to himself. I had just sat down and poured my guts out to Smitty about everything. He took everything in stride up until now except for losing it when I told him about Jay's shooting.

"So it's midnight and you're in your draws bangin' on Glover's door n' shit? Oh, that's priceless! I'm glad you put some clothes on your ass before coming here. Damn, you in love, nigga! Haha!"

"Alright! Alright! I'll admit it! I love her! Now are you gonna help me find her?"

"You know I'm down for any kind of messy shit, but what if ol' girl has already tied the knot?"

"She hasn't. At least I don't think so. It's supposed to be this weekend, either today or tomorrow. I have to find her, man."

"Know where the wedding's at?"

"It's out here, but I'm not sure where."

"Max, this ain't no Lake Charles. Thanks for narrowing the search."

"Smit, I don't have time for this."

"Just fuckin' with ya. Let me get some breakfast in me."

I needed a plan for trying to find a wedding that may or may not have been taking place in the Los Angeles area. While Smitty ate a bowl of microwave grits, I started going through the yellow pages. It was going to be nearly impossible to reach anybody on a Saturday as most of the offices that did the scheduling were probably closed. I couldn't let that stop me though. I snagged a notepad with the West-tel logo on it and began scribbling.

I had split up places to check out: churches, chapels, halls, hotels, and ballrooms. Smitty had finished his grits and sat down across the unsteady glass table from me. Being as he was more familiar with the area, he would be able to eliminate a lot of these places at a glance. A woman would have been a bigger help, but I wasn't about to bother Aunt Verna with this. I didn't know Lionel's last name and if the wedding was at somebody's house, I was sunk. I slid my list over to Smitty.

"Uh uh. Too small."

"No way. Wrong part of town for them."

"Too white."

"I dunno."

"I dunno."

"I dunno. Max, there's gotta be something she told you about the wedding. C'mon, man! Think!"

"I'm wracking my brain now. Honestly, I didn't want to hear anything about the wedding so we never brought it up much. Wait. It was to be an outdoor wedding. I remember her mentioning the weather."

"It might along the coast or something. I'm lost on that kind of stuff. Max, you *really* need a woman for this or someone with a computer. Or both."

"I wish I did. The only people who fit that description wouldn't help me do this. What about your cousin, the one who stays in the chat rooms?"

"Yeah. I thought about him. He fried his hard drive. An electrical surge or something."

"Fuck." I got up from the table and paced for a few seconds.

"Max, his people got money, right? Maybe they put something on TV about it."

"It's worth a shot." I turned on Smitty's TV and put it on one of the local channels. The news wasn't on. A commercial for an attorney promising money for injuries was going off. He was bragging about their computerized databases that would guarantee top-dollar for their clients. I rolled my eyes. I knew about this guy. I froze in mid-thought and ran to the phone.

I broke every speed limit posted as Smitty and me sped to Samir's house. I had filled Samir in on what was going down. He had already told me that his wife, Yvette, wasn't going to be happy. He was right, but she did agree to help me. Samir chose to stay home with the kids while Yvette left with us. I had a sinking feeling as I looked at my watch. Half the day was gone, and with it possibly the woman I loved.

"You know I could lose my job for letting you in here," Yvette told me as she unlocked the door to her office. I couldn't say anything so I just nodded. I wouldn't forget this.

Yvette turned off the security and turned on the power. She logged on to her terminal and then started searching for me. Smitty pulled up a chair, but I couldn't sit. I told her about the wedding being outdoors and she began focusing her search in the Malibu area for any weddings. Nothing turned up.

"Do you know the guy's last name?"

"No. His first name's 'Lionel'."

"That won't help. How about where he works?"

"He works for Barnes & Greenwood."

"*Oh*? Good company. I think they have a website."

Within seconds, Yvette had brought up the B&G website on the screen. There were photos of their top performers posted along with the names. Lionel's face jumped right out at me. Smitty noticed it too.

"That's him. That's the fool," Smitty snarled as he pointed at the screen. I think he wanted to fight again.

"Lionel *Dunning*," Yvette read aloud. "I'll bet his dad is Goodwin Dunning, the retired lawyer."

Two spaces below Lionel's photo was another face that was vaguely familiar. A pretty, young white girl. Nice tan too. Yvette was saying something, but I tuned it out as I stared more closely at the girl's photo. Where had I seen her? I started combing my memory. I began to recall the wild dream I had where I couldn't walk. It was her. *She* was the woman kissing Lionel in the dream when the phone woke me up. But why her? I was missing something.

"Yvette, what floor is B&G on?"

"Let's see . . . The . . ."

"Thirtieth floor," I said as I completed Yvette's answer for her. "Oh my God."

The subconscious memory was a mother. I always thought Lionel looked familiar. Now the light bulb finally came on.

"What?" Smitty asked.

"Yvette, you said his dad's a lawyer?"

"I said I *think* so. His dad could be a different Dunning."

"Yvette . . . You've done such a big favor for me already. I need another one. Would it be out of the ordinary for a law firm to 'consult' with a retired attorney or to try to reach him?"

"You mean 'try to find out where's he's at'? Specifically 'where the wedding is that he's at'. You've got some balls, Max."

"I have to find her, Yvette. Please."

"You already know I could get fired. You know how odd it would be to call a retired attorney on a weekend? It would be even odder for our firm to do that. *Sigh*. I'll see what I can do."

57 *Glover*

Charmaine was doing more than enough crying for everyone as she fiddled with my train. Mona had done my nails as soon as I woke up and was now finishing up the makeup. I wasn't used to being pampered, poked, and prodded, but this was to be the biggest day of my life. I was only feeling it eighty five percent though. The night before was spent up in my suite. Charmaine, Mona, and myself stayed up most of the night drinking and reminiscing over old times. Someone would say something and the next thing you know we were all crying. Tasha popped in to join us after the kids and Uncle Rob went to sleep. Even Sarabeth and Jazelle were civil and passed by to enjoy a drink or two. Maybe it was a drink or three, but I was in no shape to count. It was all I could do to watch my mouth *and* keep Charmaine and Tasha quiet in Sarabeth's presence.

I smiled my smiles to all and my eyes even watered as I looked in the mirror. My mom should have had a wedding like this. I was draped in a silk satiny-white wedding gown with spaghetti straps. The gown was a dropped waist type with embroidered pearls in the bodice. My train that Charmaine was still handling up on was cathedral style. Charmaine was already dressed, but Mona was waiting to finish with me. Ms. Stevens wanted everything in place on her when she stepped out of the suite.

There was a quick, light knock on the door. It was someone used to having doors opened for him or her. Should have known it was my mother-in-law (might as well get used to it), Adele.

"I just wanted to check on the bride," she said as Charmaine opened the door. She gave quick smiles to my friends as she darted in my direction. "Oh, you are a living doll!"

"Thanks, mom." I was straining to jump past that eighty five percent on pure force of will.

"Lionel is a nervous wreck over in his suite. I told him I would check on you."

"I'm here. It looks like everything will be going off on schedule, huh?"

"I suppose so. The guests have been arriving on schedule. I even had some of the regular boats that run back and forth reserved for this. Heh. If somebody is planning on taking a normal trip over here from the coast, they're going to have a bit of a wait on their hands. Hmm. Did you know that your makeup is uneven, dear?"

"That's because it's not finished. Mona was working on it when you came in." Adele wanted her own people to do makeup, but I pulled the plug on that. I wanted my sister by my side the whole time.

"I should have known. Glover . . . I know I rub you wrong sometimes and I apologize, but I'm wondering if we can put that all behind us after today." Adele didn't wait for an answer. She excused herself to attend to other affairs.

Mona and Charmaine finished with me except for the veil. Charmaine went looking for a pin while Mona excused herself to get ready. I could hear the orchestra warming up outside. I was to be escorted up to the cliff at the appropriate time, which was quickly approaching. I was finally alone and had time to reflect on everything in its entirety.
I took a seat in the chair and took a deep breath. Love. Humph. Was it all it was cracked up to be? The door to the suite opened again. It was Tasha. She was wearing a navy blue dress with a matching hat.

"Girl, it is sooo nice out there! I saw them bringing the doves out in their cages. I'm already out of film. Robert said to tell you he loves you and to 'break a leg.'"

"Haha. Thanks, Tasha. You are a trip, girlfriend. I'm glad we've met. Uncle Rob is truly blessed to have you."

"Thanks, niece. Um, Glover?"

"Huh?"

"I have to tell you something. Robert told me not to, but I have to. I get these feelings from time to time. My momma used to call it a gift. Robert told me to leave that foolishness alone because he didn't want anything ruining your happiness, but you ain't all that happy are you?"

"What makes you think that?"

"I dunno. Just the feeling I get. Glover, I got a bad feeling about this wedding. I mean, it could be nothin', but I couldn't not tell you."

"I'm going to be okay, Tasha, but thanks." I gave Tasha a long hug. She left to rejoin the other guests. Charmaine and Mona returned shortly afterwards.

My veil was pinned in place and we were ready to roll after a last minute check. I may have played it off to Tasha, but she was right. I had kept myself immersed in the wedding so much that I had managed to keep my heart at bay. Everything was coming to a head. I only wanted something out of life that was real for me and it was clear as Vodka that this wedding wasn't it. I loved Mr. Maxwell Guillory and I didn't think I could go through with this. With each step closer to the door, my conviction grew. I was clearing my throat to speak up when there was another knock at the door.

We all thought it was the coordinator telling us it was time to begin. No one came in. Mona let out a frustrated sigh and walked to the door. It was a delivery boy from in town. He had a package delivery for me. I guess someone couldn't wait until the reception. I signed for it and began to open the box.

A black rose was in the box with a note. Some crazy joke. It was probably from one of our co-workers. I showed the rose to Charmaine and Mona then began reading the card.

"*Dear Glover. Hope you enjoy this rose, you bitch. Because Lionel is mine and will always be. Misha.*"

Misha, Lionel's perky little friend from work. Now why would she say something like that? Unless. I'll be damned. Heh. Lionel was looking less clean in this whole twisted triangle. Looks like he had his own triangle going on.

Almost on cue, Lionel came running into the suite. His English-style tux was hitting, but Lionel was looking pretty sick. I guess he got a gift or note from Misha as well. His mouth dropped as his eyes fixed onto the note in my hand. I let the card drop onto the floor.

"Could you ladies leave us alone for a minute?" Lionel motioned to Charmaine and Mona to leave. They paused then began walking. Charmaine's eyes were asking me if that's what I wanted.

"No. No. They can stay, Lionel. We might as well get it all out." Charmaine and Mona stopped as if on cue.

"Is that from Misha?" Lionel was pointing at the tiny card.

"I think you know already." I was feeling playfully pissed.

"Baby, she sent me a crazy note too. I just got it. I . . . I . . . think she's infatuated with me."

"Go on." I folded my arms.

"She's been acting strange lately. I think she mistook my friendship for something else."

"Lionel. Don't bullshit me. I should have seen the signs a lot earlier. The way she flew out of your office that day and shit. I guess I was too busy with my own issues. I should feel better about myself for what I did, but I just feel sorrier. Misha's probably more acceptable to your family anyway. Yep. A little trophy cupcake."

"No! No! Baby, it was *never* like that. You have to believe me. Look, the wedding's ready to start. If you can just let us talk and get these two out of here." Lionel gave Mona and Charmaine a look.

"There will be no wedding, Lionel. *Do you understand*? I had reached that decision even before this 'gift' arrived." Mona's and Charmaine's mouths dropped open in unison.

Lionel forcefully responded, "There will be a wedding, Glover. Why? Because I love you and that bitch Misha is a liar!"

"No, she's not."

"What?"

Mona stepped forward and repeated herself; "Misha's not a liar."

Things had just taken a strange turn. Charmaine started rubbing her head and Lionel flew around in a spin. A deathly silent pause filled the room as everyone digested what Mona had just said. Lionel was the first person to regain his bearings and resumed damage control.

"Glover, don't listen to her, baby. Let's discuss this alone."

"Shut up, Lionel." I had reached out and grasped the table lamp near me. This caused my fiancé to pause. I then turned back toward Mona.

"And how do you know this?" I asked of Mona. Rage and immense hurt were welling up in my breast for the first time today. Lionel tried to interrupt again, but the whispered reply that came out of Mona's mouth was loud enough.

"Because . . . because. Because I've been sleeping with him too." Tears were trickling down her face. "I . . . I'm sorry Glover. It wasn't supposed to happen. You have to believe me. You're like a sister to me and I never wanted to hurt you."

Lionel seemed helpless as he looked toward Mona and back at me. He repeated the same motion several times. Damn. I was *really* clueless.

I ran across the room and grabbed Mona by her hair. Nobody was quick enough to stop me. It was too late for her. My fist rained down on her face until one eye was swollen shut. She tried to resist, but it was futile. I was about to kick her a few times when I awakened from my momentary revenge fantasy.

"G-love? Are you okay?" Charmaine had broken me out of my trance.

"Yeah, Charmaine. Never better."

"You mean you're okay with all this . . . this *shit*? With what Mona did too?" Mona had her hands on her hips and her head was lowered.

"Fuck it. Fuck them all."

Charmaine responded, "Nah! Nah! That ain't right!" Bam! Charmaine had taken her pump off and had whacked Mona with the heel. Mona went down with a shriek and was on the floor holding her head. "Now it's right."

I don't know what Lionel would tell his mother, but I'm sure it would be creative. Charmaine and me left out of the room after I ripped my veil off, but not before I planted a big, wet goodbye kiss on Lionel. Damn. He was still a good kisser. Lionel's eyes opened with surprise at first. As he relaxed and began to return the kiss, I gave him my best knee square in the nuts. I last saw him slumped over on the floor next to a cold-cocked Mona.

I pushed my way through the stunned crowd of wedding guests and out of the inn with Charmaine's help. I would explain everything to Uncle Rob and would make it up to them as well as my other guests, but I really needed some space right then. I gave my uncomfortable pumps to one of the inn staff that looked to be about my size and left bare footed. I ripped my train off when I kept tripping over it on the way down the hill into town. A tourist couple took a picture of me shooting the bird as I stormed by.

Once I made it into town, I found a gazebo near the boat landing. I found a spot in it out of public view and let out a good cry. As strong as I was, I just wanted to be held now. So many things I took for granted were completely wrong. I punished myself trying to think about how or when things started happening with Mona and Lionel. Oh, my girl. No. She was my sister.

"You tryin' to hide from me?" Charmaine had changed into a pair of shorts and a T-shirt. She had a red duffel bag in her hand and dropped it by my feet.

"You know, I joked once about what a perfect couple Mona and Lionel would make. Heh. Little did I know. Charmaine, you have any confessions you'd like to make? I don't think I can take any more surprises."

"Nope. No surprises from me. I told your Aunt and Uncle about what went down. Your Uncle Robert went looking for

Lionel, but Tasha stopped him. You plan on staying in that gown? There's some clothes in the bag."

"Thanks, . . . sister."

"You're welcome, . . . Glover."

I started unzipping the bag when Charmaine put her hand on mine.

"Oh. Before I forget. I ran into a couple of people that were looking for you. I told them that I didn't know if you felt like talking."

"What did they say?"

"They wouldn't go away. I'll tell them to come over. Be right back."

She didn't even give me a chance to say "no". Charmaine calmly strolled up the street and disappeared around the corner. I took the towel out from the bag and began wiping my makeup off. I looked at the beige streaks left on the towel as I lowered it from my face. The things women do to look good for men. Yuck.

"You missed a spot." My eyes were just coming up over the towel. The sunlight was obscuring my view, but I could make out the smile. "Scared ya, huh?"

"Wh . . . what are you doing here? How did you get here?"

"Let's just say someone told me, 'Walk boy. Walk.' and I decided to listen. You're a hard one to find."

"I wasn't supposed to be found. I thought you knew that."

"I'm hard-headed. You look good."

"You're full of shit."

"I love you."

"I love you too, Max. For real." I stood up in my ruined wedding gown and walked out of the gazebo into Max's outstretched arms. As we stood there kissing, I saw Max's little friend, Smitty standing amidst the crowd with Charmaine. Both of them were clapping and applauding us.

58 Wallace "Smitty" Lewis

Dawg, the four of us wound up gettin' tore up at Catalina that day. We even took a group photo. I keep it in a frame on top of the TV, or should I say "we" keep it in a frame on top of the TV. Charmaine and me wound up hooking up that night and have been together ever since. She's still got that ass too. Hell yeah.

My dawg, Max got hired on with that company up in Concord, but they transferred him down here after four months. He and Glover were married a year later. Incredible ceremony. You shoulda been there. The church was filled up. I was Max's best man and Charmaine was Glover's matron of honor. I was lookin' like the man n' shit, but it wasn't about me. All of Glover's people came down from Virginia including her Uncle Rob and his family. They wound up moving here to L.A. I got to meet Max's mom and some of his other people from Louisiana. Damn, those people love to drink and party. Max's mom, Orelia, and his Aunt Verna prepared all the food. I think I still got shit in my fridge to this day.

Max's cousin, Jay, wound up in a wheelchair permanently. All that shit that went down seemed to change him. He moved out on his own and is doing fine. He's back in college and on his way to earning his degree. He's also the manager at the Male Tree. He and Max still don't hang, but they talk from time to time.

Max and Glover bought themselves a nice crib out in West Covina. Believe me, they needed the room. Did I tell you I'm the proud Godfather of Max's and Glover's little boy? Yep. His name is Lionel . . . just fuckin' with ya. His name's Elijah and he's four months old. Got his dad's smile and his mom's eyes . . . and temper. Loud ass kid, but I love him to death. Any kid of my boy is all right with me.

Charmaine left the employment office just like Glover. She now works with Samir's wife, Yvette, at the attorney's office. Max tried to return the favor to Yvette and Samir by offering them both jobs with Sandifer, but they like where they're at. But enough about them. I got promoted to sales rep at West-tel. Nice ass raise. I even got rid of my hooptie. Yep, bought a brand new Hyundai off the lot last week. What's that? Don't hate on my ride. It may not be real for you, but it's real for me and that's what counts. Peace.

About the Author

Eric E. Pete was born in Seattle, Washington and raised there and in Lake Charles, Louisiana. He is a graduate of McNeese State University and currently resides with his family in the New Orleans area. *Real for Me* is his first novel and he has recently completed his second novel.

If you have any comments or wish to reach Eric, he can be contacted at: heyeric@att.net.

Eric's website can be located at: www.ericpete.com. Feel free to visit!

Give the Gift of
Real for Me
to Your Friends and Colleagues

CHECK YOUR LEADING BOOKSTORE OR ORDER HERE

❑ **YES**, I want _____ copies of *Real for Me* at $14.95 each plus $3.50 shipping per book (Louisiana residents please add $1.31 sales tax per book). Canadian orders must be accompanied by a postal money order in U.S. funds. Allow 15 days for delivery.

My check or money order for $_____ is enclosed.

Name _____

Organization _____

Address _____

City/State/Zip _____

Phone_____   E-mail _____

Please make your check payable and return to:
E-fect Publishing
PO Box 2425
Harvey, LA 70059-2425

For credit card orders go online to:
www.e-fectpublishing.com